BROKEN JAW

stories

MINOLI SALGADO

Published 2019 by the87press

The 87 Press LTD

87 Stonecot Hill

Sutton

Surrey

SM3 9HJ

www.the87press.com

ISBN: 978-1-9164774-4-5

Design: Stanislava Stoilova [www.sdesign.graphics]

PRAISE FOR *A LITTLE DUST ON THE EYES*

'*A Little Dust on the Eyes* is a luminous novel, enchanting from beginning to end.'

Robert Olen Butler, Pulitzer Prize Winner

'*An impressive exploration of traumatic loss, done with delicacy.*'

Romesh Gunesekera, Booker Prize Nominee

'*Powerful, tender and moving.*'

Abdulrazak Gurnah, Booker Prize Nominee

'*For much too long, the literature of Sri Lanka has been overshadowed by that of its larger, more boisterous cousin, India. But in Minoli Salgado's wonderful book, Sri Lanka comes alive not only as a place of mythology, tragedies, both human and natural, but as a land of dreams and of a people whose resilient spirit has a Chekovian beauty. Like Michael Ondaatje's Anil's Ghost, Salgado's work is an example of how we make literature out of the fire of near extinction. Her prose has the sublime beauty of a well-polished heirloom; something to be treasured.*'

Syl Cheney-Coker

'*An extraordinary novel of a country trying to come to its senses; to see and hear the thousands 'disappeared' by political conflict and environmental catastrophe. Minoli Salgado's delicate and determined lyricism compels us to think of Sri Lanka's missing and the silenced, always conscious of the formidable challenges of reading and writing of those displaced from us by time and tide. The result is a literary latticework of remarkable craft and subtlety that brings into*

3

focus Sri Lanka's troubled past while shaping a necessary ethical response upon which the future might depend.'

Professor John McLeod, University of Leeds

'A great book. A wonderful elegy to a childhood and country lost.'

Professor Susheila Nasta MBE, Queen Mary

for Roshan and Dilhan
with love

This broken jaw of our lost kingdoms

T.S. Eliot

Contents

Author's Foreword

Ten years ago in May, the Sri Lankan civil war was officially over. And barely seven years later, after giving a lecture on Sri Lankan writing at the University of Colombo, I was asked by a member of the audience whether I foresaw a time when Sri Lankan writers would stop writing about the war. The question made me pause. For while it acknowledged the large part played by the war in the literature of Sri Lanka, it was also inflected by a youthful frustration, almost an ennui, with its very centrality. It suggested that the subject of the twenty-six-year civil war might have been exhausted and that it was time to move on.

Would the same question have been asked of a writer engaging with other nation-shattering conflicts such as the Second World War, the Rwandan genocide or the 'Killing Fields' of Cambodia? At what point do we decide that the most brutal period of a country's history can be pushed to the literary margins or relegated to the archives? While Sri Lankan writers have written widely, broadly and with an expansive imaginative reach on subjects that side-step the war, eschewing it when it is not part of the tale they wish to tell, war remains and will continue to remain central to the writing of Sri Lanka for the simple reason that though the military conflict may be over its consequences run deep and will continue to be felt for generations to come.

This was clear to me when, after giving a reading in London from *A Little Dust on The Eyes*, a reading which related to traumatic memories of enforced disappearances in the south of the island which took an estimated 40,000 lives, a young man from the audience came and thanked me, emotionally, for writing (as he put it) his family's story, and for speaking of events that are not being discussed. He went on to describe an event too brutal and personal to relate here, but in essence it amounted to the violent death of a close family member in the south which had marked his family so deeply that it remained unspoken, an unresolved silence around which they all moved, decades after the event. He said that my reading spoke to this forgotten past and its suppression and how important it was not to forget, especially as these events were being consigned to the margins of official history in an act of willed amnesia. The encounter moved me and made me reflect further on the private and public denial of inconvenient facts and wonder what happens to all those memories that are not being passed on.

'When memory dies a people die,' A. Sivanandan has observed in his extraordinary novel of a country torn apart by ethnic nationalism. And it seems to me that the plethora of stories, novels and poems by Sri Lankan writers that engage with the political conflict mark acts of resistance to the official and public will-to-forget. For it is of course the stories that most need to be told that are at the greatest risk of being silenced.

The stories in *Broken Jaw* are a small contribution here. They join the expanding library of literature on the Sri Lankan civil war, which of course was not a singular or unitary event but made up of many conflicts with many different effects, with many different stories to be told. And though only some of the stories in this collection engage with war, all of them were written during or soon after the political conflict and are conditioned by that time.

Written between the early 1990s and 2011, they are also underscored by an exilic perspective that attempts to give meaning, pattern and shape to a home that appears to be torn apart. While the style, language and form of the stories changed over the years (and indeed some of them are written in a voice I no longer have) I believe that writing of a fractured home from a place apart during this time amplified the struggle to speak. The doubled experience of fragmentation can make trivial things symbolic, saturate and expand everyday incidents so they become dense with meaning, give silence weight. Looking back, I realize that I was trying to find a form to give language to loss, to find a home in a story while trying to find my voice as a writer as well.

This book is divided into two parts – 'Rumours' and 'Ventriloquy and Other Acts' - that mark the permeable boundaries between public and private selves. Both rumours and ventriloquy are speech acts that can deliver truths in oblique ways. In everyday life, rumours occupy the place where public secrets circulate. They expand and grow in contexts of suppression where official facts are known to be lies. And ventriloquy is, of course, an act of displaced speech. It is a means of speaking through another's mouth, of finding a voice in a new guise, of bearing witness to truths while protecting one's self and others. Rumours and ventriloquy emerge from contexts of disruption and from divided selves, testing and expanding the possibilities of what can be said. Hence while some of the stories draw on real events, all are fictionalized and displaced and speak from inside and outside history. And while most of the stories speak for themselves, a few background details may help the reading of some of them.

'A Feast of Words' was written after Sandya Eknaligoda, the half-widow of the abducted and missing journalist, Prageeth Eknaligoda, went to the Galle Literature Festival to try and publicise her husband's case and was refused a platform from which to speak. Just a couple of weeks before, prior to the boycott of the festival called by Reporters without Borders, I had addressed a closed session of English PEN in London and encouraged writers to attend the festival as it was one of the few public forums for open dialogue with Sri Lankan writers and an important space for free speech. 'A Feast of Words' was written on the day I heard that Sandya Eknaligoda had been turned away.

I have given dates for some stories, providing historical specificity to the time of writing so that it might allow you to position the events they are based on. For example, 'The Breach' was written in the final, brutal days of the military offensive when civilians were trapped and being killed in the cross-fire between the LTTE and the army in the tragically-misnamed No Fire Zone; and 'The Waves' was written after the Boxing Day tsunami and draws on the voices of the women and men I met in refugee camps for those who had lost their homes and loved ones. 'Kethumathie', a split narrative like so many in the volume, links two different historical times and is based on real events that took place in my ancestral home that is now a maternity hospital. And 'Heart' is the only piece of automatic writing I have done to date: it was written at speed in a couple of hours on a beautiful spring day in 2003.

'Heart' introduces three stories set in the countries that shaped me - Sri Lanka, Malaysia and England - that make up the fractured memoir of 'Ventriloquy and Other Acts'. Together these stories chart a journey into language that continues just as the war does in many people's minds.

10 February 2019

Rumours

Million-Dollar Wounds

Her face, I am told, has a good side and a bad side that marks the time before and after the blast. As I enter the darkness, it is difficult to distinguish exactly where the damage lies. The floor has been cleared. The wall by the shattered window has been propped up with care in a way that suggests it is recovering from something other than mortar fire. One of the effects of battle in this region is that it makes poverty indistinguishable from war. A broken roof is a broken roof; its causes are unclear. It is left to the human body to mark the boundary where poverty ends and where political violence begins. I am led to a bundle beneath the stairs and it is the good side I see first.

It carries the full glow of her face, the eye stroked into roundness by a luxury of dark lashes as she looks directly up at me, then at her father, at the altered geography of the room. She is uncertain, her reach stiffened by the bandages that run down her arm.

The cot in which she sits has been shifted into relative safety under the stairs. It contains a pink doll with painted blue eyes, her mother's shawl and her mother's smell. Her mother is gone, but the smell of her remains, somewhere in the fold of cloth, in the tang of turmeric that drifts from the stove.

She is stretching her bandaged hand to touch the doll's white hair. Her cheek dimples in dismay as she misses the toy the first time, then rounds with the delight of success as she brings the doll to her face. There is the beginning of a smile that breaks into a whimper as it meets the raw gash across her chin. A sudden turn reveals her other side, the bad side, the catastrophe where identity has disappeared into a broken skull. Half her face is missing. There is a collapse of tissue smearing her right arm.

'She thinks she came to life like this,' her father explains.

The shrapnel was so hot it fused her legs, I am told.

This is a village like any other, made up of farmers who till the land. The only thing to distinguish it is that it had remained untouched by war for so long. Intermittent flares of rumour had scattered the families from time to time, but order had returned and life had continued as before.

Then aircraft broke in and changed the colour of the sky. Helicopters and fighter jets fumed the clouds grey. Missiles scorched the horizon when government missives came thick and fast. First phone calls from the security office, then personal memos delivered by unsmiling personnel. We were instructed to leave without further delay. If we failed to do so our safety could not be guaranteed.

It did not take long for me to reason myself into the absurd logic that war invites and to convince myself that to remain would risk the lives of those we had come here to protect. But of course Thiru had known better, as all the men and women in this village had known. They understood all too well the little lies we tell ourselves to make our lives purposeful.

'Don't go,' he insisted with the full force of his arm, as we were making our way to the armoured cars that led from the back door. He was a quiet man, unaccustomed to exerting his will. The power in his hand only strengthened my resolve.

'We must.' I pulled free and saw him stumble. 'We have no choice' - though choice was of course one of the many luxuries we had.

As UN officers, we had a multitude of options: to stay and resist, to clamour for aid, insist on rights. We could even carve defences from international law that might redefine the battle lines.

'I told you to gather your family and leave. The battle is coming here. By tomorrow there may be nothing left of your village or this town.'

'We have nowhere to go.' He clutched me again, this time with an insistence that hurt. 'Sir, this is our home. There is nowhere else to go.'

The power in his hands sprang from the knowledge of this truth.

'It is better to be homeless than to risk your life!' I exclaimed. 'Go quickly and tell your people that they have to leave soon.'

He gazed at me with eyes darkened by a horror we both could see. The war had made clairvoyants of us all.

'I will be back,' I added thickly, to convince myself of the fact. 'I will come back later today if the shelling doesn't start.'

Back in the city there was little news. We were out of the line of fire. It was a relief to return to the cool calm of a hotel. I could at last release myself into the exhaustion of those final days and expand in the luxury of a foam bath. As I listened to Puccini on the radio I was reminded of my other life, the wife who no longer loved me and the daughter I dared not love.

The large events of the last week had overwhelmed our small team. We analysed and discussed the satellite images into the early hours. We scrutinized shades of darkness to distinguish between the fuzzy greys of war, the black scars of craters, the rippling blocks of vehicle installations and shifting specks of casualties. They moved like microbes following a cellular logic we did not understand. The resulting analysis blew open speculation on the kind of weapons being used. We knew the injuries would burn slowly if phosphorous was involved.

In the last days, we were being asked to verify events beyond our reach and there were too many questions - a battery of inquiry - from loud humanitarians across the world.

Did we know that much of the military hardware was

made in countries that banned its use? That we spoke from countries complicit with the war? Were we aware of our forked tongue, our culpability, our utter moral degradation in all this?

We were told to stay silent, to let our seniors talk.

But it was not the men with large handshakes who had to face up to the human appeal on the ground. It was we, the ordinary officers, who had to mingle with the villagers who came to our door.

When Thiru first arrived he only asked for grain. The rains had yet to come and the harvest had been poor. It was a time when the early casualties from a neighbouring hamlet had been brought in. The hospital so full that patients were left stretched under trees. Many turned out to be farmers who had been sowing seeds in the scorched earth. We were told they had been mistaken for insurgents planting mines.

'I will see what I can do,' I told him. 'There is to be a delivery next week.'

Thiru smiled his thanks but stayed standing at the door.

'Is there anything else?' I asked, lifting my glasses to indicate that I had other work to do.

'That,' he pointed to the air conditioner above me, 'is not safe sir. It is too hot. It is spitting hot water outside.'

I glanced at the slatted case, the dusty dials that spun loose.

'It's faulty I know. I'll get it fixed soon.'

But Thiru stayed by the door with a quiet resolve. He then raised his voice as if to make sure he was understood.

'Sir, my brother can mend it if you like. He is an electrician in the town.'

I declined the offer, but thanked him, as I was obliged to do.

He glanced at my desk, at the photo from my other life, and smiled a broad, generous smile.

'Your child?' he asked.

I drew in deeply to still my breath and stay calm.

'It is a girl, no? She is beautiful,' he said, as if such knowledge was enough. 'My daughter belongs to the same time. That is, she is the same age. And even more beautiful!'

He was laughing with a warmth that made me laugh too.

It was natural then to speak of her and to acknowledge, in passing, my need for my child. She had been taken from me by her mother, along with the dining furniture and the new TV. I ate my meals in the living room facing a blank wall for five months. While speaking to Thiru I became conscious of my child's fist curling in the shell of my palm, her fingers so soft they loosened something inside. I had wanted to curl up and sleep without ever waking up, in those rare moments of contact when I had felt whole.

I was speaking of her within the limits of emotion I could afford at the time, but Thiru stayed silent and seemed to understand more than I said.

'Our children hold our better selves,' he reflected before he left. 'When we leave them, we leave our better selves behind.'

I was late for work the next day due to congestion on the roads. A convoy of tanks blocked the traffic and caused confusion all round. A motorcyclist had been killed by a rising security barrier. Police were searching for the bike while the man's body lay on the road.

'Someone has already stolen that poor man's bike,' my driver observed.

A dead body was less remarkable than a missing motorbike now.

Moments after entering the office, I saw the sudden spark, a sizzling slash of light above my line of vision as I was approaching my desk. A crackle and the air conditioner burst into a spray of shards and jagged flames. In seconds, it seemed, my papers were alight. I ran from the room, aware only of the smell, the memory of noise.

It took me hours to restore order.

It took me over a week to accept that the photo of Louisa had been consumed by the flames.

I decided to take the small delivery to Thiru's house myself. The grain had arrived just after the storms.

'Ah, the rains have now started so you have come just a little too late,' he smiled. 'That is always the case.' He clicked his tongue in mock reprimand. Then added quietly, 'Forgive me, you mean well, but always come to us just a little too late.'

'You do not need this?' My humour became mean in the boldness of his accusation, his truth.

He shrugged. 'You can give it to someone in greater need, in another village maybe.' Perhaps the tension in my lips made him conscious of a lapse in courtesy, for he began to stutter and hurry on. 'Or you could leave it here, if it pleases. The grain is useful. Thank you. If you leave it we can keep it for another time.'

He was stumbling between words, between the sense of duty to his community and the obligation to me, stumbling as he took the jute sack and caught the white straps on my hand.

'Aiyoo,' he was reduced to haphazard emotion by the bandage strapping my wrist and palm. 'I forget, I am sorry, I forget the fire in your office, forget you were hurt.'

I was – despite myself – moved by his concern and found myself saying in a way that sounded strange, 'I want to thank you, Thiru, for alerting me to that electrical fault. I should have listened and called your brother as you advised.'

'All OK Sir, it really doesn't matter now. But your hand,' he began, as he put the sack down to examine me, 'Ah good, that is good, it heals, it heals very well. You've been lucky.

You've got a million-dollar wound.'

He was leading me back gently. 'And now Sir, do come and sit inside. I built this house myself. It is simple, we live simply, and my wife is out now. But – aha! – here she is,' his voice a bright exclamation that lit up the dank room. 'Here is my very own million-dollar gem. My daughter. Do hold her. That's it, it's alright. Every father must always hold his child like this. Hold them always, for there is nothing more precious in the world.'

He had lifted the child upon my good arm, taking care to keep her clear of the hand which had pleased him in its healing just a moment before.

'A million-dollar wound?'

'That is what the soldiers call it, Sir. A million-dollar wound that goes into the flesh but leaves the vital organs untouched. There are the regular wounds of war that break everything up, that leave you half the person you were before. And then there are wounds as rare as gems that come to the lucky ones. These wounds keep you whole inside so you can become whole on the outside too. It is worth a million dollars to have a wound like that. You have been lucky. And if you don't mind my saying,' he leant forward and whispered with a smile, 'the day you got those pieces stuck inside you, Sir, that was lucky too. That was one time when it was good you arrived a bit late!'

'A priceless wound,' I said, as her fingers folded into mine, clutching my good hand in a grip that made me slide outside myself. For there was something in the way the small body yielded against mine, in the large eyes absorbing me into acceptance, in the trusting delicacy of touch, that undid everything, broke all barriers and had me weeping for the past. I was holding a million-dollar child and making her mine.

I know I owe my life to this child who lies in the cot,

exhausted into silence by the torrent of her tears. I owe her my return to my daughter, my wife, the neglected life I left behind. I owe her my return to my better self.

And as this war continues to rupture time, split memory and break those who cannot afford expensive wounds, I am wondering at this girl whose story has been carried into the darkness of a blast, into the white heat of a moment that broke her life in two, splitting time into a good side and a bad side in a way that calls us all to account.

'She thinks she came to life like this,' her father was saying of this mermaid, this child with melded limbs, and I need to intervene and say something more.

'Thiru,' I say, lifting, yes, lifting her, so I can see the large memory of the blast expanding in her eye, 'You are right. It is a new life. But look, just look at the brightness of her eye. She sees us, she sees everything and there is a wholeness in her broken sight. This is a new life, a new way of looking at the world.'

The Breach

It had taken just two days for Sumana to master the art of flattening her body against the wall of the bund so that she was thin as could be, just a fine leaf of bone. Above and behind lay the danger. The sky sawn open by planes dropping huge exploding eggs, bullets lashed into screams, shells breaking the earth. The scramble and press of bodies. In front only the earth wall offered the possibility of protection.

Sumana thinned herself against it and kept her breath slow as another blast shook the ground and thrust more people upon her. A collective wave of panic added to her own fear. She absorbed it into the silence of an open mouth, her arms trembling down the length of her as if the earth itself had grown cold.

Cries erupted from further down the bund, marking the place where a shell had hit.

'Amma,' a man groaned. 'Amma.' And Sumana knew he would die.

For the dying always cried *mother* when about to be released, as if in sudden anticipation of the life yet to come. They never cried out for god, for water or help, for things that might offer a return to the world, but for mother: the first refuge and the last. And two days and nights before, her own mother had done the same.

'Here,' her mother had said, drawing something from the fold of her sari. 'Here eat.'

And Sumana had broken the unleaven bread and placed a piece in her mouth. She did not recognise the contact, the dry wood of her mouth against the cardboard of bread, and had chewed until the saliva came. It was the only piece of food she had eaten that day. They'd finished the small packet of biscuits distributed on a day of bounty when aid supplies got through. Ever since then aid supplies were confiscated by the men with guns.

'We are fighting for you,' they said, carrying away the bottles of water, food packets and rolls of gauze delivered by the Red Cross. 'We need the food to fight for you.'

And Sumana had looked up to see the edge of her world marked by their guns.

'Tonight,' her mother said, 'we will leave this place. We will leave for the other side where there are quiet camps. Till then, stay inside, and stay against the wall.'

It had been still for many hours. Her mother consulted the sky. Someone stirred.

'You should've gone earlier.' A woman lay slouched with a boy on her lap. She was old, or had turned old. The wrinkles on her skin rippled into the whiteness of her hair.

'Why didn't you?'

'I will wait. I can't walk. The fighting will stop. There are only so many bullets the sky can contain.'

'We can leave together. I will help.'

'No. But you can take him if you like.'

She motioned to the boy who looked at them with moons in his eyes.

Her mother lifted the child. He scrambled up and disappeared over the top as a flare opened up the sky, catching her mother in its bright star. A gust of gunfire threw her mother back so she fell warm and bleeding, pressing Sumana against the earth.

Sumana opened her mouth for words and heard her mother's fall into it. *Ammaa.*

Two days later, after her mother's body had been removed, Sumana stayed close, pressed against the earth, opening her mouth for words that would never come.

6 May 2009

The Map

Here, he said, spreading the map onto a shelf of darkness, *we were here*. His fingers lifted and traced the lines of print across his belly. He was cold, as if a damp towel lay upon him. He lifted a hand to his chest and pressed it home into a hollowness he did not recognise.

The nurse shifted and pressed something to his lips.

No. He tried to speak gently but he had lost the use of gentleness except in quiet footfalls, a leaf parting. *No thank you.*

She drew the cup away and placed it on the window ledge. Her short white dress an abstract block of light. The Major shifted in his chair.

'Udugama, we need you to be more precise. Let me fold this and bring it closer. Nurse, more light please.'

The map was lifted awkwardly - as if its exact dimensions were not known and it might suddenly expand and overwhelm them - rustled loose and quartered to a more manageable size. The catastrophe of compression, and still the map spread large across his body, rising and falling upon his chest. The angle of light - switched on and tilted - spat yellow in his eyes.

'Down, move it down. He can't see.'

And he peered at the paper searching in the forest of signs for an image that kept stroking his lids.

He had been in charge of the operation that evening, his duty to lead a reconnaissance with a team of five men in an area six miles north of the recently evacuated village of T. They had been attacked without warning and had responded, but sniper fire from another quarter had started picking off his men and forcing them back. Only two of them had made it back to base: Jayaratne, who reported the attack, and Udugama who was using the map. They now needed to know exactly where the attack took place so that they could look for the missing men and find the rebel hide-out.

This is what the Major had told him as he lay in bed looking into sunlight and wondering at the shapes that formed in his eyes. They were facts that he could flesh out into images, but the images had the substance of a dream that shifted with time, and he wasn't sure anymore if he was really remembering or constructing pictures in his head to fit the facts. All he was sure of was the map, with its neat latitudinal and longitudinal lines sectioning the fluid wildness of reclaimed hamlets, refugee camps and mobile army units. The map kept changing shape, accommodating fluctuations of ownership and habitation, but the fine regularity of squares, with their even dimensions and clean symmetry, gave a harmony to the paper that was at once soothing and annihilating. If he looked at the squares long enough, the ground seemed to disappear.

He had been tracing their trajectory on the map, evening out awkward plots of land and stray houses into an aerial symmetry that eased the discomfort of split boots and the broken brace across his shoulder. He had kept Ekenayake immediately behind him as he was new to the field and had injured his arm. Jayaratne, his most experienced man, took the rear. He was looking at the map, working in a clean square of absence, when a rattle of gunfire dissolved the lines and the grass grew savage about him. That is all he could remember. The dissolving lines and the loss of bearings.

He now looked at the map, trying to focus on the specific space he had been working in last, but the tangle of written words kept getting in the way. He traced them with his tongue unravelling the twine of letters - *Tellippalai* - he said, hoarsely, releasing ripe berries of sound.

'Can't be right, that's miles from here.'

Vettilakerni, he continued, drawing a reed of music from the page, *Puthukudiyiruppu*, into birdsong, *Madhu*, a gasp,

Bogamuyaya, Vadhamarachchi, Mullaitivu, Killinochchi.
The names were delicious and tangy as they tumbled from
his lips. *Murukandy, Valvettithurai, Kankesanthurai.*

'Stop, man. You're rambling.'

But he carried on, compelled by the joy of enunciation,
the taste in his mouth as he savoured the rich combinations
of sound. And as he did so the names drew themselves into a
garland of hidden logic as towns, villages, churches, lagoons,
rivers coalesced into a history that cannot be contained in
history books. He was oblivious to this, delighting in the new
game. But for the men and women who were gathered round
the bed, he was breaking all distinctions. His incantation
was releasing names from regularity and calling into being
places where homes were burnt by torchlight, where workers
disappeared, where children played with a ball that tore
off their feet, where the husks of empty boats drifted into
sea. And when he had exhausted this section of the map he
moved east to a hard cluster of Ks, *Kattankudy, Kalmunai,
Kokkadichcholai ...*

'That's enough, Captain. Enough.'

He stopped, the words tightening into knots about his
throat. His mouth felt dry. He stared at the paper, watching
its creases rise and fall across his body, moving as he breathed.
And then, unbidden, the image returned, and he was back
with his men again.

He remembered the white spray of onion flowers first.
They had just passed a field - a field of onion flowers - when
Ekenayake indicated that there was something lying on the
ground. So he had walked over to have a look, keeping his
men on the path in case the field was mined. He was conscious
of crushing the onion stalks and of the white flowers brushing
his boots. He was about to turn back when he saw her.

She could not have been much more than child. Her long
hair had been pulled back and was spread in an arc about her

face. Her clothes were torn and there was a bright red gash about her neck that made the flesh hang open in a grin. He breathed so fast he was sure she was breathing too. Then, desperate to do something, he reached for the map again to record the site of the killing. There was a crack of gunfire and he heard a couple of men in his unit respond. His hands weren't free. The last thing he remembered was seeing the words on the map unravelling and the girl's hair spread among the onion flowers as he ran into sunlight.

Flowers, he heard himself say. *There were flowers in her hair.*

Brushstrokes

They had taken the trouble to spare his hands. He bore the marks of their frenzied imagination in a welt of wounds, but they had left his hands smooth, clear but for a tinge of colour at the tips.

They had redesigned him so he would never walk again or stand upright, sit, blink or defecate without carrying the knowledge of their power inside him. And of course they had had to do something about his face. It was sure to be a distraction to such imaginative men. He had once been good looking - 'Looking good!' his mother would say before he left for work – and although electrocution, not rape, was the sexual torture of choice, you could never be sure with such imaginative men. It was a disappointingly straightforward matter to rearrange a man's face.

Yes, they had taken the trouble to spare his hands. As he shifted his shoulder up the wall and brought his fingers to himself, he felt the contrast: his fine, tapered hands against the ridge of shattered ribs.

'Out!'

He was struck forward and staggered into light. The sun dazzled. It broke in stripes of light and dark from behind the pillars, so he did not see the shadows pacing the yard, just heard the shackles of shuffling feet. At the end of the corridor a door opened and he was thrown onto the floor. Smooth, dry, cool cement spreading along the length of him. A comfort that calmed his broken cheek.

'Up!' He was struck behind the knees. Felt a screeching white light, heard a gasp and felt the livid flecks in his mouth. Another blow upon his back lifted his face from the floor.

'Up I say.'

His body tore purple as he twisted and found himself facing

the long edge of a desk. His body turned traitor, extending the pain.

'You are a very lucky man. One of the fortunate few.'

The voice was thick, lush, creamy. His interlocutor had eaten and drunk well.

'You must know,' the voice continued, 'just how lucky you are.'

He was still staring at the lash of light that ran along the desk, looking at the bubbles of wood that marked the place where varnish had congealed.

He was trying to steady his mind, brush the stroke of light before him into language. One of the things he had learnt under torture was the power of words. There were words that could extend the pain and there were words that could save you. Your own words led to trouble. Their words were good. If you repeated their words, you might just survive.

'Yes,' his mouth broke into blood. 'I am a very lucky man.'

'What's that? Speak up.'

'I am,' he rasped, 'a very … lucky man.'

'Good, good, he understands,' the well-fed voice chortled. 'See deputy inspector, they know when they're on to a good thing.'

'Yes, he's hit the jackpot. Won the lottery big time.'
The deputy flicked the bamboo switch across his heels and sniggered as he flinched.

Words can hurt you, they can save you, they can even bring back memories of a lottery win. As he lay there, he was taken back to a moment in the past, when he had felt the afternoon heat on his face as he ran from school with the delight of new coins jingling in his pocket and seen the lottery seller's perambulating booth, when he had bought four tickets for the New Year.

'Here Amma, for you,' he'd exclaimed as he burst in the door. 'To bring you luck this New Year.'

'Oh, you are naughty boy spending money on such things.' His mother had ruffled his damp hair and then squeezed him with joy.

That was the year they'd won enough money to buy their first and last car.

He had been her only child, her little piece of gold. Her lucky, lucky boy. She was with him now, holding him, as he lay on the floor.

'Here lucky man, have a look at this,' said the well-fed voice, 'they say you're something special. Have a look. Not bad, no, for a man who skipped school.'

He did not, could not move - just wanted to stay there with his mother's hand in his hair - but a flash of colour compelled him to look up, to turn his chin against the pain of a broken jaw. He was facing the shimmering brightness of a painting that was being held in front of him. It was familiar, one he recognised, one of his. He knew the spray of crushed amethyst that he had sealed on the subject's cheek, he knew the delicate strips of newspaper that made up the man's clothes. It had taken him six months to put together this portrait, to get the depth of colour and texture just right. To match the gem dust with the skin tone, the paper to a sarong. Six months of labour to honour the man who bought him his first paints. Six months for a portrait that would take pride of place in the National Gallery. This was the one painting they had not yet destroyed.

'What kind of art do you call this, mixing everything up. They say there are even crushed garnets here. Why do you waste precious stones on this – this picture of what? This man, this nobody, he doesn't even have a name. Who is this, this "Teacher"? This Teacher you've made look like a king.'

To name him would have marked him, led them to a neighbour's door.

'Who is it, hmm?' A boot came down on his neck,

loosening teeth, the pressure releasing a whistle that seemed to come from somewhere outside.

'Lost for words, eh?' the boot struck him. 'Do you not know how lucky you are? Come speak. You are lucky.'

'Yes. Lu – lucky.'

'How lucky?'

'Lu-lucky.'

'Then why,' soothed the well-fed voice, 'do this? Not just for this nobody but all the nobodies in the state. Nobodies without names. "Teacher", "Potter", "Bather" – you think these people make your country and it's right to throw gems in their faces. You call yourself a multimedia artist and then have the gall to ...,' the voice struggled for control, 'you have the utter impudence to draw our Leader in a cartoon! A precious painter for the people but a cartoonist for a king! Cartoons in charcoal, drawn in three-four lines!'

So, It was the cartoons that had brought him to this. He had been warned not to offer them to the press.

'Three or four lines. I can show him three or four lines.' The butt of a gun was pressed against his chest.

'No. Leave it,' the man held up a cautionary hand. 'We need to deliver him tomorrow. Take him away and tidy him up. We need to get the materials. The Leader wants a bright picture, the brightest of all.'

'OK, Lucky. Off with you. You're the only scum artist we've spared. Be sure to give thanks when you pray tonight.'

His painting was carried before him till he reached the end of the corridor. It was thrown upon a bonfire that blew smoke into his cell. He saw it spit violet in the flare. He was then taken back to his cell and thrown onto the damp floor. He gathered his limbs about him to still the trembling inside.

He could not recall when the world had first come to him as a clash of colour. When he had first felt the wonder of release of a stick upon sand. When crayons came off in creamy rainbows upon a wall. When the world came to him in a clamour of interrupted shades. When he brought different elements together and his pictures came alive.

Critics later claimed it must have been an inheritance of sorts. His father, an uncommon thief, a man of improvised creations, and his resourceful mother who could mend tools with thatch. They said these skills must have been passed on and that their poverty helped.

But it was not poverty or desperation that led him to add depth to broad strokes. A fish, a cart, a bird gathering flight. They needed the warmth of coconut leaf, chillie dust, the sparkle of a granite chip in hot tar. And his mother, who adored him, had complained affectionately at the time.

'Stop sniffing around my curry powders, child. The ants are already nibbling up the rice on those pictures.'

Where others saw chaos, a neighbour had seen his hidden world. His Teacher who brought him paints and cartridge paper, wood blocks and coal. His Teacher who had never taught him anything but the confidence to carry on.

'Remember all you need is about you. The world is your colouring box.'

And so it was. The gem cutters in his village offered the best scraps of all.

'Here, wash,' a guard came in and tossed a bowl to the ground.

They knew he couldn't stand at the tap anymore.

'Soap, clothes. Dress, eat.'

In the lapse of time, his body came back to him as a collage that allowed him to order himself. It was good to be able to separate the different elements of pain. To distinguish the broken jaw from the cut above his brow, the ribs that splintered into rawness from the breath that came as a thin strand. If he lifted his legs slowly, he could feel something drag in his back. He could just about flex his right wrist, could just about control the movement of this hand. He was still looking at his hands when he heard footsteps on the upper floor.

A door grated open and closed. The generator juddered into life. It was time for the inmates above his cell to learn to speak the right words. He could see the colour of their cries in the room when he was brought to an improvised studio the next day.

Everything was arranged before him as if an operation were to be performed. The canvas upon easel, the brushes arranged in order with bright tubes of paint. The bottles of varnish and oil, scraps of cloth, spices, seeds, and of course, his trademark - delicate boxes of glittering dust. The official portrait of the Leader, beaming from the height of the presidential balcony, blazoned in the national colours of maroon and white from a wall behind. They had anticipated his needs, these imaginative men. As he was helped to the stool it would have been easy to believe that they actually cared.

'You are to paint the Leader. Is there anything else you need?'

'I would like water. And a toothbrush.' The first words that were his.

The guard looked discomfited. A toothbrush was not what they had in mind. The inspector pursed his lips.

'Get them.'

The items were duly brought on a tray.

'Anything else?'

'Just the shutters. A little less light.'

They drew the shutters down and sealed the door.

In the hours that followed, he found that he could break

through the pain. He built textures and colours from the broad sweeps of the brush. The movements came naturally. He selected materials with ease. For it was a delight, a release, to offer himself to a portrait like this.

He knew all too well the arched eyebrows, the broad jowl, the black slug of the moustache. The five fat caterpillars that came from the raised hand. Had drawn them all too often in the clear strokes of cartoon. He knew the features well and knew how to gather the materials to life. To get the density of greed, lust and cruelty in the glint of dark eyes. And yes, he would use the gem dust they had brought him, the quartz and tourmaline. Draw the elements together to create the right shade of green. He would pinch pepper seeds into place, blow coal dust, cast oil, feel his strength grow. The pain inside broke into raw streaks of paint. There was a large release of power when he completed the face.

He was not aware that they were watching him and he would not have cared. For just look how well he had begun to drape the Leader's form! Resplendent in national dress, just as required. See the long streams of white cries screeching down, falling in perfect folds of open anger towards the feet, the electricity passing through into scorched shadows that burst in a spray of fire from the raised arm.

How well he has captured the shimmering wetness of blood of that red scarf that drapes the broad neck! This is the first time the Leader has been brought to life like this.

As he went on, slashing the figure into life, the imaginative men stayed watching in awe. For they too could see that it was a great portrait of the great man. It was exactly what was wanted, brimming with power. It contained dark lashings of colour that magnified his form, threw him into height. There was searing authority in that raised arm, a spreading confidence in the expanse of teeth, a visionary sharpness in the chips of eyes, and the clothes were perfect down to the lengthening detail of the red scarf.

It was a portrait that they all knew would stand the test of time. A fitting tribute to the Leader, a work of power and strength. And this man, the insurgent artist whose body leapt like a wild star, must surely be brought out and showcased to celebrate their altruism and artistic reach. For they were imaginative, civilised men after all.

It didn't matter if people saw the bent man scream as he raised his arm to show off his work, and if his arm stayed locked in this position as he continued to cry out. It didn't matter if critics murmured at the vicious brushstrokes and the lashings of dust, if there was a stray grub in the varnish, if they saw crimson as blood. And it didn't matter – why should it? – that, despite his disfigurement, people were drawn to the strange smile that came from the gash of his twisted lips.

The Dictionary of National Humiliation

The entries are coming in so fast I am having difficulty keeping up. There are just two or three days left to complete this task, before this last note too will be added to the list by someone else.

Perhaps Jayali, who sits quietly in the back office, will take on this job after I am gone. She has been watching me as if I'm a ghost these last few months.

I have called it the *Dictionary of National Humiliation* so there will be no mistake about what's happening here: how all the entries mark the depths to which we have sunk.

It is not in alphabetical order. I abandoned this plan when I realised that 'An Abduction at … ' belonged after 'Death Threats to …', though my initial system had its advantages in offering a numerical basis for analysis. In the early years, death threats outnumbered the abductions but now it is the other way round.

Instead I've listed everything in the order in which things have taken place, or were thought to have taken place, in the hope of giving a sense of continuity to our broken times.

We are desperate for this – a sense of cause and effect, a sense of accountability – something that will release us from the arbitrary violence in our midst.

Truth has been curtailed for so long that we have started to doubt our very eyes. And the book is patchy, I know, there are gaps and elisions where conjecture might take hold, but in the loose arrangement of facts connections *can* be made.

This is an underground past. Officially nothing of what I say is recognised. Officially it is as if I even might not exist.

Let me explain what is going on. Let me be absolutely clear.

Ever since our late editor's article appeared in the press and gained international recognition as an exceptionally prescient piece of journalism, identifying the ills in our country and predicting the manner of his own death, people have been writing as if they are already dead.

It is an insurance policy of sorts as you cannot, of course, put a dead person on trial, kill them or do any further harm. The only way you can harm the dead is to sully their name, the memory others have of them, the narrative they leave behind, and this is where my book comes in.

People write what they know, or what they have knowledge of, be it the circumstances of a murder or corporate bribe, a sighting of an abduction, a neighbour's vigil with armed men, and do so freely knowing that if they come to be killed for what they know and say, their innocence is marked by the permanence of the printed word.

'In the event of my death ...' is unnecessary for we all die at some time; rather it is 'In the knowledge of my death ...' that seems to be the condition of writing every story. The necessary starting point for a person to write.

'In the knowledge of my death, I write of ...' 'In the knowledge of my death, I bear witness to · ...' 'In the knowledge of my death, I testify that ...' The pieces vary in the details but the collective story is consistent. Each sentence is simultaneously a death sentence and a testament of truth: this writing is both an acknowledgement and an erasure of guilt.

It has come to this. The times we live in corrupt us all. Perhaps writing of what we know and writing ourselves out of the picture is the only way to get to the raw kernel of facts. The individual loss of ego is necessary to mark our collective past.

I am nothing outside this book, my life suspended somewhere between the pages of death threats and abductions, so I find I am writing myself into a future that has already been written. If you are reading this, you are reading - no, listening - to one who now only exists in words.

Jayali is impatient. She glances through me at the open window and sighs a long sigh as if the breath coming out of her is inexhaustible and she might disappear through the window.

But nothing can clear the smoke. The ceiling is scorched and I can still feel the warmth of the flames that sputtered into life as they torched the office, setting fire to curtains, files, tables and chairs. They did not see me of course – how can they see what they do not acknowledge? – as I slipped from the room with the unbound book pinned to my chest.

I do not officially exist. As a renegade writer I have no markings, no citizenship, no bearings, no home. I do not need to be abducted to be made to disappear.

Only these words mark my existence. This dictionary unlocks the past. If you are reading this, you too will need to choose – fast! - between silence and speaking out.

Either way, you would do well to write everything down. Just in case, you understand, they say that you, too, do not exist and are made to disappear.

Summer 2011

A Feast of Words

for Sandya Eknaligoda

The writers were at the table, eating each other's words. Delicate morsels of sliced crime, tangy segments of romance, silver spoonerisms washed down with a glass of iced humour that turned the lips green.

'How delightful', one cooed, 'I must try this at home.'

The wine critic was not sure. She would like to have sampled some rough shreds from a local saga of lost lives, but didn't want to be first. She settled for some pickled irony instead. She might fold the saga in her napkin and eat it later in the leisure of her hotel room.

The book feast had been almost everything she'd hoped for. An orgy of words, with whale watching, devil dancing and fire walking between meals. The initial fuss that the feast was inappropriate, when the rest of the country was half-starved, had died down. Only a Nobel Laureate and a Booker Prize Winner had cancelled their meals. It was not much of a loss. She had tried their work and found it went poorly with Bordeaux.

But the local saga with its siren-red chunks was a different matter. And so were some of the short shots of poetic violence that she'd tried that morning. A caffeine kick, those poems made her wake to where she was.

She was about to reach for the saga when someone staggered forward with a dish too bizarre for words. A giant black and white cartoon of a man's face slashed by a cross of two chillies upon the lips.

'My husband,' said a woman, proffering the placard and a sheaf of printed leaves. 'This about my husband who's gone. Please take and read. Read and eat at same time. It is possible no?'

'It's inedible.' 'It's uncooked.' 'Where's it from?' They all asked.

'My husband,' she repeated with a hunger they did not understand. 'He was a writer like you but disappeared last year. He wrote words the government did not want to hear.'

A plate of silence was served that made them feel hollow inside.

'What words?' offered the wine critic. 'What words did your husband say?'

The woman shook her head.

'His words have gone with him. That is why I am here. I am looking for him in your feast of words.'

31 January 2011

Breaking News

It took one full hour for my brother to realise that a plane had crashed in his back yard. I don't know to this day if this information was of any use to him or not. I used to tease him for being slow on the uptake, but when it took him many minutes to answer the phone I knew there was something wrong. He normally answered my Friday calls promptly as he didn't want to miss the News.

'Sorry', his voice sounded hoarse. 'I can't find my torch. There's a black-out. The power is off.'

Power cuts were common, particularly during the dry season. I'd just mentioned the possibility of drought when he broke in.

'Did you hear that?'

'What?'

'The gunfire. Searchlights are sweeping the sky and the gunfire began just as you started to talk.'

I paused and watched the LCD display on the alarm clock flip to 6.15. There were popping sounds through the line and then, silence. My brother was some five thousand miles away and some five time zones ahead, suspended in a future that I had yet to reach.

'It must be an air attack. Wait, I'll check the internet.'

I always kept my computer close to hand, permanently connected to broadband so I only had to click Refresh to find out the latest. Ever since the World Service had suspended broadcasts to the island and a policy of violent intimidation had worked to silence media critics, the only reliable source of news had been supplied by an anonymous underground movement that lived in the island and wrote directly to internet sites. These unknown citizens made it possible to get a sense of what was happening. I was scrolling down the entries when my brother cried out and a dull thud boomed down the line. Something solid rolled on the floor. He had dropped the phone.

'You alright?'

There was silence. Then more popping sounds. An entry from Reuters confirmed that unidentified planes had been spotted coming over the city a few minutes ago.

A snuffing, slippery noise and he was back on the phone.

'God that was close.'

'You OK?'

'Yeah. The house shook. There's a fire outside.'

Another report: anti-aircraft fire over the city, tracer bullets strafing the sky. I gave him the news and clicked for more.

'I can't see much. It's too dark. But the sky is lit up with something. God, this smoke is something else.'

'Hey, wait.' I was in control. Reports were coming thick and fast online. I could communicate what was going on and prepare him for events.

'Yep, definitely hostile planes. The air force has scrambled interceptors. They're over the city now.'

'I can't see anything.'

'Wait, let me see if it's on Breaking News.'

I put the phone down and turned the TV on. The rolling news channel was still rolling on the news it had given earlier in the day. Then the anchorman interrupted to say that reports were coming in of an attack over the city and anti-aircraft fire. A strip of words sliding along the lower length of the screen confirmed what he had to say.

I walked back to the phone and lifted the computer on to my lap.

'Yep, they've confirmed it. Hostile planes over the city and anti-aircraft fire.'

He was silent.

'Isn't it great I can tell you what's happening.' It was good to be able to help like this. I was the older brother. I was used to giving advice. 'You really should get broadband. You wouldn't need to depend on local news and rely on my checking things out.'

He remained quiet just as I clicked open a picture from a new report that showed the city sky lit up by the broad beam of a searchlight that cut the blackness above buildings into a cracked pane of grey light.

'It looks dark out there. All the streetlights are out.' It seemed natural to be describing his world to him, to be calling it into being. I was entering this world when he began to move somewhere else.

'Hey, remember when you broke Thatha's computer by spilling water all over it and I took the blame?'

Trust my brother to remember irrelevant details at a time like this!

'Yep.' More reports were appearing on screen – from China, Israel and the island itself – giving different numbers of planes. I opened them up in quick succession, trying to mentally condense the news so I could pass it on to him. Some said there were just two planes, others said up to four. One report said that an explosion had been heard at the airport.

'I told Amma the truth. But Thatha never let me on the computer after that. I've hated computers ever since.'

'There's been an explosion at the airport.' I was clicking through the entries to find out more.

'Anything else?'

'Nothing yet.'

'Well, I want you to know that I forgive you.'

'For what?' This was crazy talk when his home was under attack.

'For stopping me working on Thatha's computer when it should've been you.'

I could tell when my brother was upset and I could tell when he was joking. The inflection in his voice told me he was joking now.

'You're welcome.' It was necessary to humour him, to keep his spirits up. 'But wait,' another entry lit the screen, 'they say the explosion might have been a bomb. They're closing the airport.'

I heard something smash on the other end of the line.

'You OK?'

'Yes,' he wheezed. 'I wish I could see what was happening. The smell is awful. I need a drink.'

'Don't worry. There's more news coming in. I can tell you what's happening. There's one report here that says a village was attacked from above. They might have dropped a bomb before coming to the city.'

'Which village?'

I gave the name.

'Never heard of it. Anyone hurt?'

'No casualties yet. It says they are diverting commercial planes to India because the airport is closed.'

'Ah,' it was a long sigh, of relief possibly. 'I would like to go to India. Perhaps I could go this year. Would you like to come? We could travel together. Just the two of us.'

'Yes, planes are being diverted. And it says it was not a bomb but an unauthorised plane from behind enemy lines. It says an enemy plane crashed at the airport and there are no casualties apart from the pilot.'

I continued giving him news of events as they were happening and he stayed listening and talking nonsense of the past and his future plans. I was telling him that the enemy planes had been shot down, and one renegade report had said it was a kamikaze attack, as I moved from the computer in my bedroom to the TV in the living room and back again, until it seemed as if I was doing all the talking and walking and he was just listening and being still.

As I spoke of what I read and heard and conveyed it all to him, I began to feel as if I was making it all happen, as if the crashed planes and explosions and broken buildings that were being reported only became real as I spoke of them. His long silences and increasing distance from it all set him apart from the darkness and the smoke that began to enter my room, so that when a report came in that a plane had crashed in his neighbourhood, onto the building next door, it seemed as if it had happened in my own home and not in his back yard at all, and when it said that there were no casualties to report, I was indeed master of the event and could make facts bend to my will, stand tall amid the detritus about me.

The LCD flicked to 7.15, a quarter to one in the morning of his future. Sirens blared and shouts came down the line. I was called into the burnt shell of his home just as a new report flashed on screen. I found myself reading aloud to him of a casualty in his neighbourhood, in his street, in his house, who was not a casualty but in fact the first fatality, the first civilian fatality, who had died on impact from the crashed plane, an hour earlier.

I knew this report might be wrong because others were in coming in, and I said as much and assured him I would read them all, for he needed to know what had happened and was happening between all the possibilities that were opening up to him now. It was especially important, I felt, for him to know if he had died or not.

'There are conflicting reports,' I continued as the phone spat and crackled on the floor of his room. 'One says there are no civilian fatalities, the other says that at least nine people have died in your neighbourhood. What do you think, Malli? Do you think someone has died?'

But there was no time for him to answer. Reports came like artillery fire. I found myself struggling to keep up, reading on and on, rushing so fast that I hurled headlong before the reports even came on screen while the hours between us slid, slipped and suddenly collided in a flash somewhere above his roof.

They say I was talking without sense, talking for some time, after the thickening smoke had obscured all the words from sight.

22 February 2009

Too Many Legs

'Sinhala leg or Tamil leg?'

'Doesn't matter. Put it on the Tamil pile. There are too many Sinhala legs.'

'How many have we got?'

'9 Tamil. 19 Sinhala.'

'I should move one. We can't have odd numbers. We need two legs to confirm a body.'

'Can't do that. These ones are officers. People will find out.'

I stepped over the ticker tape and was counting as they talked. There were indeed 19 Sinhala legs, all trousered in police khaki. I made a note of the number and moved on to the Tamil pile where the disorder was more tangible in a mangle of sarongs and slippers. A burned hand fell open in the middle of the heap.

It was just another bomb blast but I had been lucky this time. I was in the next street buying a lunch packet when the boom took hold. I could make precise notes, despite the dust, and get them back to the office in time for the afternoon news. Years of censorship had skilled me to fire words like blanks. I noted time, place and number, then stepped aside to let someone pass. He tore a sarong from the Tamil pile and rushed to bind the legs of an injured man who was screaming at them to do something. Sirens blocked out his words. I could only make out the shouts of those sorting out limbs.

'Hey look, we've got a Muslim!'

Another leg thudded on the pile.

I went to the injured man across a drain of running blood. He was shouting for his son who'd run off to buy sweets just before the blast.

'He ran behind,' he said gesturing in the direction of a policeman who stood sifting through the rubble of a former teashop. The policeman lifted a wedge of corrugated iron.

'Found it!' he shouted. His colleagues rushed forward but I was in front and got to the bomber's head before the others did.

It was an astonishingly beautiful head, lying on its side, cleanly severed where the cord carrying the cyanide capsule might have been. A plait of hair was coiled on top. The girl about fifteen, eyes open wide on the face of a boy who lay by her and seemed to look back at her in a moment of stilled time. It was as if their bodies had dissolved in the gaze, *as if they recognised each other in that last instant of life.* I felt the warmth of the words as I wrote them and had to cross them out.

Recognition indeed!

I tallied up the body parts and went back to the office, pausing to tell the injured man precisely where his son lay.

Releasing Marius

She writes about the man she sees walking along the beach, going nowhere. It doesn't matter that he looks aimless because he is dead now anyway.

He is walking by the shore.

It is five in the afternoon.

His footprints are washed away by the spreading arc of the waves. His presence a mere gesture brushed by the ocean's erasure.

He sweeps an imaginary fly off his elbow and adjusts his sarong, passing a fold of cloth between his legs and tucking it behind his waist. She sees his face as he looks down. There is something familiar about it. She thinks, too late, that it might be Gregoris, before he extends himself into the water and allows it to swallow him, leaving the beach clear except for two empty catamarans and some coconut shells.

It had been an unrealistic night. A heavy, purple moon. No stars. The huge waves reduced to a crush of lace.

She had sat on the balcony, as usual, writing her diary.

A moth settled on the page. She brushed it off, watched its skittish flight, and then saw a glare in the distance beyond the fringe of coconut trees.

By daylight there were a few huts here.

At night the landscape and sky were sealed in darkness.

Now there was a harsh haze of yellow, illuminating nothing but itself.

An unrealistic night.

Gregoris had heard the stories, the narratives of rupture, but when the motor vehicle drew up outside his home while the moon was at its height, and he opened the door to strangers who took his son for questioning, he could only ask *Why?*

and look to his wife for an answer, as she cried and clutched her child with a force beyond her size.

They prised her off Marius. It was just routine questioning. They would release their son soon if everything was in order. Marius turned and looked at Gregoris with eyes slashed with fear. Just a few moments earlier the lad had been asleep on his mat. Gregoris lay down on it and felt the warmth of his son's body blend with his. The door swung open and shut all night, but no one came. His wife howling like the sea.

They did not dare look at Gregoris the next day in case his bad luck rubbed off on them, but they embraced him like a brother and murmured their prayers. The boatmen belonged to a small community of fishermen who believed in miracles rather than fate. They carried amulets around their necks and saw the future on the horizon, where the belly of the sea met the belly of the sky. They could read the unseen, the weather to come, and what lay beneath the waters of the ocean.

They looked out and saw crimson - the sign of a rich yield - but strained to look further, beyond the buried sun.

Jacob looked up and did not know if he should say it, did not know if it would be wise to tell Gregoris that he had already heard a helicopter stuttering seaward that morning.

Brother, he said, laying his hand on his shoulder, *I will come with you to the police station. They can manage without us today.*

Sure brother, you go. It's best to act quickly, they all said, but Gregoris was quiet, breathing deeply.

He found comfort in being with them, passing the rough rope through his hands. He could already feel the curve of wood press his shoulder as he pushed the boat out, feel the water lash his knees, the suck of sand swirling by his feet. It was a ritual of connection that made him feel whole.

I will come as I have always come, he said.

She would part the curtains at dawn and watch the boats emerge, a casual gift from the sea. They would appear as one and then part like two slices of a crescent moon, the oars rising and falling through the water. In the distance, the tiny dots of polystyrene beading the nets, and two figures splashing in the water to drive the fish back. Gregoris had revealed all this to her. The sun would lift then, in seconds it seemed, drawn up by the nets from the sea.

She parted the curtains at dawn, but there were no boats in the water. They had landed already and had been left. The sun lifted up without anchor.

They brought Marius back straightaway, lifting him free from the net like a child. His wounds were clean. He looked asleep. They rolled the nets and laid the ropes out, walking up and down the sand in single file.

Gregoris stroked his son's head, smoothing his hair, and rocked him back and forth to give him life.

They sat down and waited for him to stop.

Jacob ran on, calling, crying, to Gregoris' hut to let his wife know that Marius had come home.

\

The Waves

And so the stories surface - thrashed on shore - and we reach to curve them to us and preserve what we can of the lives they contain.

There were three waves, each charged with a different pulse. The first a purple appetite, the sea reaching towards unhistorical huts and colonial forts, tentacles uneven floors and lifts thatched sleeping mats into surprise.

It reached our knees and rushed out again, sucking back for about a mile. We saw the sea bed appear and our children ran towards the exposed rocks to play.

The second a high electricity of noise. My husband called our third girl and I grabbed our baby and ran out to see a mountain surge towards us, felt water lift my feet to flight and carry us towards railway tracks that disappeared as we approached.

This baby and I were as one body lifted and dashed. A rocking horse, a chair, broken walls of driftwood crashed against us. Bones buckle, my arms full with a child's howl that swallows the sound of waves and swirls into dizziness.

I remember my two older daughters running towards the rocks. That last picture keeps coming back: their long legs running with laughter across the exposed sand.

I never called them back. I never called them back.

I call and call them now but they keep running on.

And then the anomaly: *I somehow found a strength I did not know I had.* This the common element in those who lived long enough to remember.

When the third wave comes, sea and sky are one. The horizon expanding so the future swells to meet us and I break free, torn from my body into a new power.

This is what happened. This is all I remember. There are the moments before and those after and the fragment of time that pitched us into a new landscape. Listen to us, write it down, before we run dry of words.

It is all that is left. These bones of words.

I repeat: *The waves came. Everything is gone. The waves came and everything is gone.*

There is a man who - every morning - returns to the planks that were his home to guard them from human scavengers. *They are mine. They are all I have now. But they are mine.*

In his pocket he carries the lock of the door that was swept away. Keeps it safe against his chest. This memory. This pride of ownership.

There is the woman who on seeing the first wave draw back told her family to run, run fast, because the gods had been disturbed, but who, despite this, ran in the opposite direction, back to her house to get her children's birth certificates, then heard the second wave approach and knew that identity was not important any more.

Her husband who has asthma sits looking into a distance beyond the sky where water continues to swell. His illness meant he did not learn to fish, to trust the waves as the others did.

Another man cries, *Thank god it happened during the day!* and throws an arm about two plastic bags that contain the gratitude he salvaged in the sun.

Talk to the two women who were trapped in their house, the swirling tides sucking around the walls and sealing them in till they were released by a neighbour who opened the door and let the demons in, demons who still swirl inside so they cannot feel their mothers' thin touch. She is alive as a ghost to them. She looks at me with mild flowers in her eyes. A gentle woman sitting still by the bright flames of her grown daughters.

A large extended family gathers round this hearth. They find a rough comfort in being together.

The men look defeated.

For generations they have sifted the waters with their long drag nets, nets that scallop around each boat, linking them in harmony. They will never go to sea again, never go to sea. But they do not know what else to do. The chain has been broken. Their history ends here. And in eyes swept clean of hope, so it seems does their future.

The doctors come twice a day to dress the wounds and dispense aspirin. The nuns bring trays of rattling sweet tea. And I, powerless to flesh the bones into narrative.

Around the trestle tables children gather and draw pictures of waves and clouds meeting and houses swept into trees. *Look sister, look at my picture. My grey crayon ran out so I had to use black. What's that? Will you take a photograph of us, please?*

I draw my video camera up and see a cluster of curiosity dense the lens. White smiles and white eyes. Shining children silvered by the sea. I zoom close and then swivel round and pull back to capture the baby in her mother's arms, the mother who kept repeating that everything is gone, see her give her breast to the baby as her husband strokes the head of their other five-year-old daughter - this family who lost two daughters to the sea.

I swoop towards them and then draw back to contain the others in the room, then zoom forward one last time towards the infant crushed against her mother's breast, swoop so fast that all I catch is the curled fist on the white blouse and the curve of the mother's upper arm, catch in that sweeping grey instant, a close up of a tight, tender, knuckled grip.

1 January 2005

Getting to No

His habit, on returning home, was to kiss her on the lips before going upstairs for a shower. Hers, to submit, and then call Sriya to make the tea. It was a cursory greeting which, like so many of the exchanges in their marriage, had dwindled to little more than a brush, a glance, on desensitised skin. But it served a purpose, this small connection, and always helped.

Today, as she went to answer the door, Saro felt a heaviness that made her take a little longer to reach for the key and turn it. She could not have named it, this feeling that weighed down her shoulders and seeped into her legs, and put it down to tiredness, though from what she couldn't say. As she opened the door she saw him leaning on the doorstep, tapping his knuckles against the wood, beads of perspiration swelling at his temples. He checked her face, the subdued eyes that lifted expressionlessly as she raised her lips, and walked, chin-set, straight past her to his room.

It was the first of many slight changes. As the days passed she noticed that his natural silence had congealed. He would read the newspapers, holding them up as if to screen himself from her, his back stiff with resistance, like a soldier. The meals to which he had always sat with a whisper of a smile, were now eaten deliberately, each mouthful a convoluted operation of alternate grinding and chewing from side to side.

'Is it alright?'

He continued chewing, studying the plate in front of him, his shoulders hunched over the table.

She hesitated.

'You don't have to eat it if you don't want to. There's some vegetable curry on the cooker.'

He remained silent, jabbed the last forkful into his mouth, rose scraping the chair against the floor, and went to his room, still masticating a mouthful, clicking the door behind him.

She waited in silence, listening to the susurrating suck and swell of waves upon the beach. The sea, with its easy rhythms, brought a steadying calm upon her during the day, but on evenings such as these made her restless and ache to get away. She stared at the plate with its violent smears of gravy. The glass, smudged with his lip prints. A few stray grains of rice had fallen on the floor by his chair and she bent to pick them up, squeezing her fingers against the tiny beads and placing them carefully onto the plate. They left small spots of grease, like the tell-tale prints of crushed insects, which would need to be wiped clean before she went to bed; ants were drawn to even the tiniest residue of food. And then she saw the fine scratches on the floor by his chair. Parallel swirls that made her think of the scouring prints that she had, as an untutored wife, made on Teflon pans. She would get Sriya to polish them away tomorrow.

In the kitchen the pots squatted, pregnant and accusing, about the sink. They had acquired thick wedges of grease about the rim and the coconut-milk gravy was beginning to separate. She tipped the chatty pot that was half-full of potato curry and began spooning its contents into a blue tupperware container. They settled into the container, reaching the edges like an invading army. It was his favourite dish, potato curry, yet he had hardly touched it, eating instead the beef curry that she had got Sriya to make hurriedly when she realised the fish had not thawed. What a waste, she thought. What a stupid waste.

She turned on the tap, touching the spurting water with her fingertips to make sure it was hot. It choked and spat before settling into a steady stream. She dipped each pot gently in water, before wiping it in clean broad strokes. Her face was splashed with this water that smelled of chilli and onions and soap. And as she cleaned she remembered that at one time it had given her a curious unqualified pleasure to know that the face he kissed each evening must smell of these things. She had wanted him to know that she was part of the house that sheltered him and that Sriya, whose smirk and chatter made her frequently create excuses to send her from the house, was nothing more than a temporary presence whose withdrawal confirmed the permanence and security of her own care.

Sriya had gone out for the evening. The kitchen was hers once more. After washing, she cleaned the work surfaces, sealed the bin (ants would collect here too, given the chance), turned off the gas, secured the windows and the garage door, and switched off the hall light. When she went to the bedroom his eyes were sealed and his arms crossed over his chest like those effigies of knights she had seen in English cathedrals. Silent, inviolate images of death.

During the night, the thoughts that she had kept at bay through the activities of the day would seep into her consciousness, prising her from sleep, while the sea with its insistent hiss and slow withdrawing sigh seemed to breathe into her ear. And she would look at her husband, watch the rise and fall of his chest, hear the grating of his breath, and feel that it was he who was keeping her awake, and hate him for it. Nothing seemed to disturb him. Not all the elements combined into an earthquake, storm and fire, could rouse him once he closed his eyes.

Sometimes, however, when she returned from the kitchen, he would still be reading, his glasses sitting solid upon his face like a screen. She would go to the bathroom, brush her teeth and begin to undress, always aware that he was not really reading - his breathing was too quiet, his body too still - but coldly studying her. She was on guard then. Would turn her back on him and avoid looking at him directly.

Often, too often, he would wait till she was pulling the sheet back to get into bed and then quietly, studiously, put his book down and look straight at her. She wanted to ignore this but knew she could not, that it was tiny actions such as these that demanded, compelled, attention.

'Is it a good book?' She managed a smile. Tried to relax.

'Alright.' He shifted to his side, splinters of light glancing off his glasses.

She would delay then. Turn, sit up and start brushing her hair, teasing out each tangle to the tip.

He would continue to study her and turn the pages of the unread book. She pretended not to notice. Pretended she was used to this attention, that she was just being watched, not netted. Finally when she could delay no more, she would slowly put down her brush and reach once again for the sheet. She felt overwhelmingly tired. The muscles in her body ached and her mind cried out for the blind oblivion of sleep.

He had removed his glasses now. His eyes, small and puffy, were holding her. In one full look he was making his claim upon her. There was no point in delaying. She climbed into bed beside him. A moment's pause. Then his fingers, gentle but insistent, would begin to stroke her hip.

'You must not do it if you don't want to,' Dr Veena, her unmarried college friend and only confidante, had said. 'Make clear to him that you don't want to. You must take responsibility for your own sexuality. If you don't someone else will. He only gets away with it, you know, because you let him.'

It had sounded so simple, like a clear blade cutting through the tangled skein of silences and half-hints in which she and her husband had become enmeshed. She thought of the authority of Veena's voice, her bulky comforting arms, and remembered her mother whose warmth and soft-soled calm she now longed for. What would her mother say to her now? She tried to resurrect her, felt her approach gently, saw her smile a strained, knowing smile and then, as the darkness descended, disappear into the shadows, saying nothing. There were no answers there.

And so it was that one night when he had been in bed leafing through a book on estate management she confronted him with it. Peeling back the bed sheets, she looked at him steadily, and began to speak with a tentative playfulness.

'Why is it that I can tell from your expression that you want to make love?'

He relaxed into a smile with what appeared to be genuine warmth. 'Mmmm.'

'Look I don't mean to be difficult - try and understand - but I really don't feel like it. Do you think we can wait for another time?'

If she had not known before, she knew with certainty now that he despised her. This was not mere disappointment. A scowl skewed his features before he had time to rearrange them. He sighed heavily, restraining anger, looked away and cut her out.

She could not bear this. It tore her. This last chance at intimacy wiped out.

'Please don't. I'm sorry. I'm really sorry.'

She sidled up to him snuggling her neck into his back.

'OK. Let's try now. Please.'

But it was too late.

And he made her pay. Day after day. Rejecting her advances, not speaking, not looking, not touching. Eventually one night he felt her and she submitted, hoping for some tenderness. But none came. He was angry. It was functional. She felt used.

She began to feel she was at fault and wondered whether after so many years of marriage it had come as too much of a shock that his wife was unhappy; whether she should have told him sooner. But no matter how hard she tried she could not fully convince herself that he did not know of her reluctance. That one of the unspoken rules of their marriage was that she would make herself available to him when he needed her. And, without meaning to, she became careless of her appearance and began to neglect the house. The floor remained unswept for days, leaving grit that stuck to their soles, the laundry collected in puffy bundles in the bathroom, a thin skin of dust and dirt settled on the furniture, tea stains collected on teacups, fine cobwebs hung languorously from the ceiling like powdered lace whilst she, Saro, the district administrator's wife, read magazines in the garden dressed in a tatty sari. Even the bold-faced Sriya was shocked.

One day the kitchen door opened and Sriya strode out. A strong odour of red onions and garlic swept into the garden with her. Sriya stopped, pensive, scratching one foot with the other, searching Madam's face to see what mood she was in. Saro sat expressionless, feeling for a loose pin in her hair with one hand whilst leafing through some pages with the other. After a moment she looked up to see Sriya's powdered face and clean dress. Her hair, Saro noted, was smooth and shiny with coconut oil and had a small cluster of jasmines in it.

'So where are you going?' she asked flatly, trying to hide her relief at the prospect of being left on her own.

Sriya relaxed. She would not have to ask Madam's permission this time.

'To my aunt's at Mirissa.'

'And how is your aunt keeping,' Saro said, shuffling her slippers onto her feet and getting up.

'She is well, Hamu.' Sriya hated this ritual of question and answer.

'Well you can stay out for the night. I will not need you till tomorrow morning.'

Sriya flashed a broad smile. She liked this change in Madam. Dinner had not yet been prepared and here she was being given the night off.

'Will that be all, Hamu?'

'Yes that is all. Enjoy yourself.'

Saro saw Sriya return and leave by the back door,

negotiating her wicker basket on one arm. She watched her walk sturdily down the road past the corner shop and disappear towards the bus depot.

The house appeared fragile now. Isolated and unsteady. The walls, painted a brittle white, were flecked with small betel-red tiles and streaked with whispering grey trails that sparkled with sea-salt. It seemed to her that this house which was her home was nothing more than a broken bit of flotsam spewed out upon a shifting landscape of wind and waves.

She turned around, turning her back upon the house, and walked slowly towards the sea – a surging argument of blue beneath a thickening sky. She continued to walk steadily and began to feel her slippers sticking to the sand as she approached the water. She teased them off with her toes and noticed the imprint of her feet embedded into them like thick shiny skins, until a swathe of sea water lifted them from the beach and drew them away. She watched them float, bobbing ridiculously one after the other, until they were drawn apart and a huge tongue of water engulfed them.

The waves were lapping her feet now, the border of her sari was damp. She looked down. The muslin fabric appeared translucent when wet and she watched the translucency spread from her ankles to her knees and up towards her waist as she walked on.

She reached forward arching herself upon a wave, enjoying the luxury of coolness, but suddenly, with a sharp pull, felt herself being dragged away from the shore. The sari, saturated with water, became immeasurably heavy, trapping her legs and frustrating her attempts to swim. She kicked out and threw her arms forwards but it was as if the lower half of her body was bound up and pulling her down. Her legs buckled; her hair, now loosened, kept sweeping forward sticking over her eyes as she struggled and thrashed for balance, thrusting her neck forward to keep her face above the water. She was exhausted, being carried several yards from the shore. It seemed to take all her strength to stay afloat as she tugged and tore at the sari which confined her. Then, involuntarily, she swallowed a few gulps of water and felt a sickening trickle flow up her nostrils, cutting her off.

It was her last chance. Drawing her body into a fine pulse of energy, she pushed herself upwards from the heavy glue of water and broke through the surface. She took a full breath of air and lunged forward, using her arms to propel herself towards the shore. It seemed to take lifetimes, each stroke a mustering of her individual will, each intake of breath an elemental defiance, until she felt the sand underneath her and collapsed upon the beach, her throat burning.

The sun had begun to set. It cast a lurid light upon the house, burning its pale walls a hot red. Saro drew herself up, exhausted. Her shoulders ached as she flexed her arms behind her, pressing her palms into the sand. She stretched her legs and felt their weight against the waves. She felt herself expand and fill her skin.

Her husband, she reflected, would be returning from work soon. He would let himself in, have a shower, and not notice her absence till his dinner was due. Then he would walk into the kitchen, find it empty of dinner and cook and wife, swear, stride into the garden and maybe, just maybe, he might see her sitting on the beach by their home, watching the sun slide quietly over the edge.

It was entirely up to her now.

Father's Will

It was scary going back and confronting the past. It was like walking into someone else's motion picture, straying into another person's dream. He was aware that he had started to hallucinate on the drive back. Everything came in slow motion. Even the figures on the road appeared kaleidoscopic, like floating particles of coloured dust.

He turned from the car window and closed his eyes. Philip would be back by now. He held on to that. As they entered the drive, he opened his eyes and the house that he had not seen in years appeared to burst into flower. Crimson, yellow, white. He was home.

Philip has aged and the woman who now enters the room is a stranger. Alma, father's second wife. She eases herself into a chair and adjusts the folds of her sari, brushing off some invisible crumbs. Philip taps the ash off his cigarette and draws in deeply, studying me across a spiral of smoke.

'Two hours earlier,' he says, ' and we would have arrived at the same time. My flight was held up in Dubai.'

'I know. The driver told me. How's Laura?'

'Fine. She's in Boston right now. Some conference on gender and war or something.'

Alma cuts into the conversation.

'Now children,' she begins in a voice stronger than her frame, 'tomorrow is going to be a busy day. I need to make a number of calls and arrange for some lunch packets. We can't cook food in the house till the funeral is over next week. You can do what you want in the morning, have a lie in if you like, but I want you here in the afternoon. Your father's executor is coming to sort out a few matters. He will need to speak to you.'

She is brisk, dry-eyed; an empty glass.

'Who is he?' asks Philip.

'Dr Landenburg. A friend and your father's last doctor.'

Father. There is something about the way she says it that frays the nerves.

'There can't be too much to sort out.' Philip says wryly.

Years of comfort peel back in his yellow smile. The brother with the sleek watch upon his wrist and good food in his belly. This beautiful old house festooned with flowers and the scent of incense is a crumbling old shack to him. I find it hard to like him though I am glad he is here.

'I think I'll go for a walk.'

'I'll join you.'

I had hoped to be alone.

The red drive scintillates with feldspar and chipped quartz. I used to cherish these stones, gather them, wash them in a bowl and lay them out on a towel to dry in the sun. Now I walk on them and pretend I don't see, feeling them scrunch under my shoes. Philip folds his arms behind his back, walking straight and tall. We look as though we own the place, but neither of us knows quite where we are. We've reached the wall and find ourselves facing a new macadam road, new buildings, new people and noises of the day that defy translation. The traffic is a large argument. Even the birds screech like cars.

'There used to be some trees here, and a fruit stall. Do you remember?' says Philip. 'That chap who sold mangoes. He was always chewing betel, then would try to spit at crows. Betel stains everywhere. Father was always shouting at him to move on.'

Father with his red face and stubbly chin, swinging the bottle in his hand and roaring words of fire. Mother drawing her thin arm through his and motioning him inside. The retreat into darkness. I don't want to call this into being. Focus instead on the movement of vans, trucks and motorbikes that blare and hiss, cutting us off from the house behind us.

'It's a different country.'

'Yes, we got out at the right time. Thank God for mother. Otherwise we'd have been brought down just as he was.'

Philip. Polished silver. I admire and fear his certainty. Feel petals of doubt unfolding everywhere. Father's pain, his concentrated fear drawing him taut and tall into a fine line of solitude. It was easy to draw away from him while Mother called *Philip, Lee, you're all I've got now, my darlings.* Her warm form folded on the stairs.

'My god, look at that!'

Across from us, at the end of the road, stands a huge fuchsia building draped with a large shiny banner, *Galactic City: Shop in heaven.*

'I am sure that is where Evan Amerasekera's home was. He must have sold up. Got the right people. I understand land is like gold dust round here.'

Yes, Philip would approve of such a move. *Why do you want to live here?* he had said when he came to my basement flat in Streatham. I had moved since then but knew what he would say if he saw my new café-flanked apartment, so had never bothered to invite him. And he, in turn, had kept away from me.

'It's hideous,' I say. 'I'm going back.'

Philip goes on ahead. I walk in the opposite direction and get completely lost. A woman at a bus stop directs me back home. She smells of stale sandalwood and I am conscious of the rope of hair brushing her blouse. By the time I get back, Philip is already on the veranda, helping himself to some fried rice from a paper packet.

'Damn these flies. I'll have to eat inside. What took you so long?'

I remain, out of time, watching the darkness descend as the night crackles into life. Crickets, toads, mosquitoes, geckos. The hot percussion of the dark.

Alma is somewhere and everywhere, shuffling around, turning off lights and shutting doors. She wants to lock up and I wonder if she always did this, whether in their life together she was the watchful one.

'His last days, were they happy, do you think?' I am trying to imagine Father thirty years on, adding lines to his face, grey streaks to his hair; but he refuses to age, resists my touch.

'Your father had changed. He wasn't the rough diamond you remember. He had taken to painting and was even trying yoga.' Alma is smiling and clicks her tongue. 'You know I'd even find him standing on his head some mornings. Yes, he was happy. He knew he didn't have long.'

She is about to say something else, checks herself. 'You should get to bed. You've had a long day.'

But I am not ready. I need to hold the night at bay. Delay the walk through the house, the return to the old bed with its smell of naphthalene and soapsuds, delay falling into dream, into memory, delay waking up to a cut-glass morning without Father in the house, this house in which every shift of the curtain contains his footfall. For the first time in my life, I find I miss him terribly.

'Don't worry. You go. I'll lock up.'

I do not like her easy ownership of him, his house.

∞

Daylight. When he wakes he feels the skin slide off his face like sheets of ice. It is cold. It is 82 degrees in the shade.

At first I don't recognise him, the tall grey man who is opening a bottle in the kitchen. The shock of hair, grey eyes, aquiline nose and thin lips. Then the young man who was Philip slips out from the sliced laugh.

'Well, well, what did you get up to last night. You look like the devil himself. Here, Alma's left some fruit for you. Try the small bananas, they're great.'

Alma, the small woman in the photograph who has now walked into my life. The woman who is treating Father's funeral as if it is a business arrangement.

'Alma. Right. I've been meaning to ask you Philip, what do you think of her?'

'She seems OK. Quite calm, you know, but then anyone who was willing to put up with Father must be a pretty solid sort. I like that sort of strength. Wish Laura had it. Why?'

'Nothing. She just seems a bit too ... detached. I know he wasn't easy to live with but I guess I had assumed that they loved each other.'

Love. I am now talking to my brother about love.

'Oh lord, you're a sentimental bugger, Lee. I'd forgotten that. Who cares why they married? It suited them and that's that. What we need to make sure of is that Father didn't leave everything to everyone he set eyes on. Not that there's much left of course. Just the house, land, and a few bits and pieces. But you know what he could be like. Never could keep anything to himself. We should find out more when this Landenburg fellow shows up. Here, eat up. Try and take it easy till he comes.'

The jakwood table. Its small bevelled drawers and leather surface with circular indentations swirling on top. His father's pens, a fist of needles in a jar, and some old, faded copies of National Geographic. A pair of his father's sandals lie tucked underneath the table. He pulls the chair back and sits down, observing the imprint of heel, sole and first three toes on each of them.

There is a canvas rolled up in a corner where the table rests against the wall. He picks it up and unfolds it and looks at the painted human figure against green. It is a woman. The brushstrokes a flurry of feathers. She is laughing, holding a hat in hand, shading her face with her free arm. It is a picture of his mother. He knows it is her for he has seen the sepia photograph upon which it is based. His father painting from a photograph, his hand dancing on the canvas that extends the reach of his arms.

He lifts his hand and touches the grained colour. The brushstrokes under his fingertips come to him as sticky kisses of paint. His hand is resting on his father's; something surges inside him and breaks. He is blind with an untold longing and goes crashing outside through crimson, white, yellow. He has rushed headlong into Alma who is laughing and holding a stranger's hand.

'This is Dr Landenburg. He has come to talk to you about your father's estate.'

Philip draws himself a chair. This is what he has been waiting for. Alma composes herself on the sofa and studies her feet.

I am furious with images that don't make sense. I want to leave, find the place where they are now washing him, changing him, combing his hair, cleaning his nails. I want to hold his hand and ask him why, why, why he never wrote to us after we left, why he never sent more than just one photograph - it was of Alma, his new wife - why he never asked to see us - did we mean no more to him than the baggage Mother took with her when she went? And what am I doing, allowing myself to be drawn into this charade of civility with three people who would never have gathered together under one roof had he not died?

But something is wrong. Alma has looked up and Philip's face has swelled with anger. Landenburg has settled back in his seat and continues in his soft voice.

'So it's really quite simple. No estate duties or administrative charges. Alma can see to it.'

'Preposterous!' Philip blasts, and rises to his feet. 'I knew he was financially inept but this is absurd. Don't tell me I was dragged all this way for nothing. I won't have it. I'll contest it! Show me the papers.'

'What's the matter?'

They all turn to me.

'He's just given everything away that's what!'

I have never seen Philip like this.

'Your father,' says Landenburg, handing Philip a bulky envelope, 'has bequeathed his entire estate to a children's home in Gampaha. Alma has the life interest to the house.'

'That's it?' I ask.

'Yes.'

'Well then, as Philip said, why call us over?'

'Alma did not know what was in the will. He only discussed it with me. This is as much of a surprise to her as it is to you. How do you think,' he says, leaning forward as if to see me better, 'your father should have disposed of his estate?'

For the first time I find I am looking straight at him and see a gaunt man of seventy or so with a shock of white hair, dark glasses and a full beard. He is dressed in a deep black suit that is too big for him and that is shiny with starch. He looks sinister, a man of contrasts, and I want to hear his voice again.

'Pardon?'

'How do you think your father should have disposed of his property?'

The voice is husky - barely above a whisper. No wonder I had not heard him before.

'Well, it's his, so he's free to do what he likes. What I don't understand is why - if you had the slightest inkling he might do this - you called us over here. It's not as though you had any reason to believe he'd leave us anything. He never got in touch.'

'Precisely.' Philip folds up the papers and crushes them into his pocket. 'Didn't care for us then, doesn't care for us now. Well I won't let this matter rest. You can count on it.'

'And what would you have done with the house if it had come to you?' Alma's eyes are points of fire.

'Why sell it of course. It must be worth a bob or two. Developers are crying out for an estate like this.'

'And what about you, Lee? What would you have done?'

I don't know. I hadn't thought of this. My home is in England now. I have become a stranger here. Can't find my way about. But I had always carried the memory of this house, the time of wholeness, inside me like a secret pocket, and returning to its cool folds, the dark arches and swaying fans, I have almost started to feel complete again. All I can be sure is that -

'I love this place,' I say. 'I would never want it changed.'

Philip walks towards the veranda, his back turned to us, and lights a cigarette. A few white blossoms fall onto the porch.

Landenburg coughs, strokes his beard and his voice seems to emerge from the shadow of his chair. 'You know, your father did try to get in touch but your mother did not want it.'

'How do you know?' Philip speaks without turning or showing his face.

'Soon after you all left, he wrote to you,' Landenburg is looking at me but I cannot see his eyes. 'Not once, not twice, but many many times. There was no response. Then after six years of writing, writing to the dark, there came a letter from your mother. She made it clear that she didn't want to have anything to do with him. She said the letters upset the boys. Asked him to stop. So he slowly lost heart. But deep down, you know,' he removes his glasses, 'he never lost hope. He hoped that one day, when you were old enough to understand, to reflect upon the way two people can sometimes drift apart, that you would get in touch and return. It was what he wanted most of all ...'

His eyes are translucent with cataracts, misty with another time. And I don't want to know what they are telling me, want to shake this raw remorse that shrieks, telling me that all my pinched reserve and carefully-crafted schoolboy stoicism was wasted, a sham to conceal another sham; that my weeping mother, who I cradled like a child, was a liar and a cheat; and I don't want to know, and hate him, when he says the words that remove all doubt and send me hurtling towards him like a hurricane - 'to see you both again before his death.'

'Left it a bit late though, didn't he?'

Philip sounds faint, weak, or maybe it's just me, for I am not hearing well, just looking into the old man's eyes which draw me into spirals of grey, down, down, into a time when I washed stones and found my father's hands in the bowl, the muddle of his hands in mine as we scrambled for stones, giggling, and I looked up and saw him looking back at me, white with laughter, with joy, with pure bright circles of love, just as he is looking at me now.

Sassy

'We want sassy,' the Editor drawled. 'We want quirky, clever, up-beat, something that people can come curl up with after work and forget the office, the washing-up, bills, the divorce. We want witty, warm, racy, something spunky, assured, at home in the world. A book that makes no apologies. *White Teeth. The White Tiger.* Now, those are the novels to look at.'

'White teeth?' she said, looking hard at the lips that creased into a small rose as they drew on a cigarette.

'Yes darling' - cloud flowers bloomed - *'White Teeth'* or *The White Tiger,*' and the lips split to reveal a wedge of yellow. 'Books that made their mark.'

She was silent.

The Editor crossed her legs and leaned forward and tapped her cigarette over a small saucer.

'We do not want,' she said, sliding lashed eyes between the stack of files on her left and the telephone on her right, 'bleak books.' (The words a slap on each cheek.) 'Nostalgia' (extended nasals, like *neuralgia*) 'does not sell. It is so' and her voice teetered on the precipice of disdain, 'last century.' (Safe-landing.) 'All those women looking back and wondering where they belong as if it was of earth-shattering importance, all that searching for roots, for identity, for place, when all they have to do is get out and mix a little. We are not into passive women, books of reflection, or stories of despair. They are so passé and' she inhaled once more, paused, and exhaled, *'so slow.'*

Rings of smoky lipsticked 'o's reverberated upwards and popped in delicate gasps.

'Give us sassy and we will think again.'

She went back to the house, a small terraced place in a county town which had a view of a castle keep from the top window. She never thought of it as home, for she lived elsewhere, returning each night to her family five thousand miles away. Not that these visits were confined to nights. She would manage to get back during the day sometimes when nobody was listening or looking at her too hard. She was, essentially, a traveller, shuttling between worlds and times, between states of living and dying, in suspension, neither here nor there. It might have posed problems for some, this living and dying at the same time, but it was all she knew and she had grown used to it. It was *certainty* that confused her, made her panic, as if someone were squeezing all the air out of her. She could only breathe in the climate of change.

She returned to the house and peeled off her clothes, folding them in a pile on her bed. It was the first thing she did when she came back, this shedding of the clothes that held her in place. She slid into a track suit and went to the kitchen to boil a kettle.

Sassy. That is what she needed. To be sassy. She wasn't quite sure what it meant, only that it was evidently not her. She was not-sassy, that's all. Sassy negated like an unexposed film. She stirred herself some Horlicks and went upstairs to look up sassy in the dictionary in a crazy logic of negative affirmation. She was directed to other continents, other time-zones – sassy: 1856; West African believed to be English for saucy; an African tree with a bark that is an 'ordeal poison'; the poisonous bark of the tree.

So sassy could be ingested, absorbed like the Horlicks in her mug. It was a decoction of sorts that might transform her into a better writer, an alchemy from somewhere in Africa, the one continent she had never visited and knew almost nothing about. Perhaps she might be initiated into Sassiness by drinking sassy juice, become Sassy by rubbing the oil into her skin, look Sassy by dusting herself with the requisite bark powder, and for this she would need to travel further than she had ever been in her life. Further than Culpeppers or

Beanfreaks in the nearest city. Further than the internet with its inexhaustible, cyberspatial pharmacy. Further even than the cave-dwelling medicine man in the Sinharaja rainforest who it took several days' travel by – respectively - train, bus, bicycle and foot, to see for the reward of a phial of herbal oil, a cure-all for everything from elephantiasis to haemorrhoids, gangrene to anamnesia. No, this was one journey she had never made before. Little wonder Sassy had eluded her. She had been moving in the wrong direction all along.

She began her initiation by watching an old video of *Absolutely Fabulous* some three hours long, followed by the best of *Goodness Gracious Me, Friends* and *Sex and the City*. She read Fay Weldon, Jackie Collins, Jeannette Winterson, Danielle Steele, Angela Carter, Edwina Currie, Zadie Smith, Jilly Cooper, Helen Fielding, Salman Rushdie, Meera Syal, and Hanif Kureishi, until sassy people held endless multilingual conversations on sex (gratuitous), politics (peripheral), culture (high, middle, and no-brow), relatives (the living and dead as well as the living dead), growing old (and how to stop it), diets (endured), affairs (imagined, thwarted and real), war (the Third World War and war in the Third World), shopping and cuisine (interchangeable), fashion ('it takes just one woman to start a fashion'), bodies (their own and others and the otherness of their own), literature (their neighbours, friends and ancestors), over a five course dinner in which Chianti, fondue and asparagus took precedence, before shedding their identities along with their clothes and indulging in an orgy that lasted six weeks and ended up with them all appearing naked before a supreme court judge who happened to be ex-Britain's ex-Prime Minister's ex-wife.

At the end of this congested confabulation of the confederation of the culturally cognizant and confident, this peripatetic prosopopoeia of repartee that led to a month without sleep, she was utterly exhausted. She went to bed and pulled the covers over her, enjoying the delicious disintegration in the dark.

And this was her undoing. If only she had managed to stay awake she might have made it. But here, in the infinity of soft blackness, she was betrayed into herself. She was home again, the only home she ever knew, the place where she coincided with herself once more. It was a place beyond description because no else had ever been there. Others like her may have made their own homes: each was unique beyond words. Here, fragments of her history slithered into life and embraced her in unholy union, dissolving the sharp dichotomies of a present lived in a separate space from the past. In this space, she was able to sink into the landscape of her mind and disappear into all the people that she might have been – selves containing all the possibilities within her, selves discarded like sequins of skin on the long road that brought her to the terraced house in the county. She absorbed them all. And she was free.

When she woke the next day she had the familiar sensation of being bodiless that always came upon her when she had slept well. The experience of wondering where she was and who she was, the experience of being just a smooth dark slate of sensations. Then the sickening containment of time and place came upon her, and she recognised the limits of this body on this bed in this room in this house. She was a person again, individuated, just one of the many she might have been, and she knew now, with complete certainty, that she was not, and never would be, Sassy.

She went downstairs to pick up the post and found four A5 envelopes splayed upon the mat like a fan. She glanced at them, recognised her own writing of her own name and address and did not bother to find out who was sending her work back. Then she registered a mechanical drone of sound that seemed to be coming from above. A strange noise, both human and electronic. She tip-toed to her office, the noise swelling as she climbed the stairs, and pushed the door open.

Her office had been cleared, books stacked on shelves, and files stood to attention against the walls. Her notice board, with its babble of scrap paper, had been removed and in its place were monochromatic posters of Che Guevara and Hitchcock's *Rear Window*. A copper mobile twisted by the open window. A blue vase of speckled tiger-lilies gleamed on a cabinet by the door.

But it was her desk she did not recognise. Shifted away from its corner by the window and placed squarely in the middle of the room, it seemed so much larger and aggressive, dominating the space, while the person who sat at it, her glossy hair folded into a French plait, polished green fingertips clicking at the keyboard while the radio throbbed to an unfamiliar beat, was someone she knew immediately though she had not met her before.

'Hi,' said the woman standing up to shake her hand and smiling broadly to display a perfect set of white teeth, 'I'm Sassy.'

Sassy kept herself busy so there was little contact between them. Sassy wrote relentlessly, churning chapter after chapter without interruption or anxiety, and her social life was correspondingly intense. Swimming on Mondays and Wednesdays, gym and zumba on Tuesdays, tennis on Thursdays, dinner with friends every Friday and clubbing on Saturdays. Sundays Sassy reserved for herself – that is for her facial, body scrub, bikini wax and pedicure.

Sassy loved loud music, phone calls, and food. If Sassy wasn't singing along to the radio, she was on the phone chatting to friends, or serving herself another portion of coriander rice with curried monkfish followed by interminable cups of strong black coffee. The smells were as delicious as the music was loud, and the house that was not her home became increasingly strange, a place of ordered activity, of song, laughter, of languages and odours she could not translate. Her bed was no longer her sanctuary, for the darkness was punctured by Sassy singing, Sassy laughing and Sassy in the shower. Sassy seemed to have the knack of duplicating herself, occupying all the main rooms at once.

The change forced her to retreat. She sought refuge in quiet corners she had not noticed before. The utility room which led to the back yard, the closet by the front door and, quietest of all, the cellar she had not been in for years. Here, in a darkness and silence deep enough to sink into, she found a kind of peace. The floor was feathered with soft shavings from pine tea-chests that held the scent of crushed leaves. Cobwebs, sticky with sweet insects, edged the walls like lace.

While Sassy worked upstairs, she made a nest for herself in the cellar. She brought her books down and read them by the light of the paraffin lamp she found in the garden shed, tracing the words with her fingertips as if absorbing them into her skin. She brought her food down here too – the scraps Sassy left in the fridge – and preserved any left-overs in the empty yoghurt tubs she had not the heart to throw away. She got used to the permanent dark until she began to fear the forms that emerged in the light of day. She would eat little and often, nibbling morsels with relish, and then stroke her hair with care, teasing out stray bits of dirt, and curl into the comfort of newspapers drawing them close about her shrinking form. The hair on her skin thickened her into warmth. She began to relish the heat of the water pipes that ran along the length of the cellar wall. The darkness effaced time, seasons, even memory, absorbing and accepting her as she was.

All might have gone well if she had kept out of Sassy's way. One day the inevitable happened and she came face to face with Sassy for the last time.

Sassy, she knew, had been completing a book. She had heard the telephone calls and seen the post, confirming that a contract was on the way. She had managed to steer clear of her during this sensitive time. Then one morning (it could have been afternoon, she only remembers the slats of light that fell on the cellar steps) she heard Sassy walk downstairs to the floor above her and felt the front door open and close. She was hungry so she made her way towards the kitchen to see what she could she find to eat, when she realised, too late, that Sassy had not left as she had thought, but was standing right in front of her, slicing herself some rye bread.

She was smaller now, having eaten only scraps, and she paused hoping Sassy would not see her. But Sassy saw her, screamed, and flicked the bread knife at her missing her head by a whisker. She leapt down the steps and curled up tight behind a trunk in the cellar. Someone slammed the cellar door and she was sealed in.

She had no idea how long she remained there, tracing the walls, searching for a way out. She was only conscious of the hunger scratching lines of pain down the length of her body. There was no food left in the pots, not a crumb. Eventually the pain curled up inside her and sent her to sleep. She woke as the door opened and a sharp block of light fell on the floor. She scuttled into the dark as the stranger came down with an object in her hand. She smelled the food before the stranger put it down: coriander rice, with extra spice. Sassy must have made her some.

Thrilled, delighted beyond measure by this unexpected gift, she leapt forward reaching the plate in one bound as the stranger raised a long arm above her. The arm extended by a wooden mallet came down hard in one blow. The last thing she heard was a voice that was terrifyingly human.

'Rats!' it shrieked, as darkness fell once more.

Solitary Reaper

'Towns should grow like mushrooms,' my father once said, sipping his evening beer while watching the sun sink like a ripe pomegranate into the sea. 'Organically, over time.'

We'd been discussing the village constructions that had been taking place inland. They were part of an island-wide government initiative to improve the lot of landless fishermen who still lived in wooden shacks perched just a stone's throw from the waves. My father had settled back into his cane armchair and closed his eyes, leaving me to wonder at how towns might grow like *mushrooms*, those fleshy creatures that I had only seen erupting like a skin disease in my illustrated copy of *British Flora and Fauna*.

Looking back, I realise he might have been preparing me for my long exile even then, domesticating the world into Englishness. Ever since I had started school he had been replacing fragrant Jaffna mangoes with shiny apples at tea time, and pronouncing in stentorian tones the opening lines of Wordsworth's 'Solitary Reaper' – *Behold her, single in the field, Yon solitary, Highland Lass …* – as we sped past stooping women who stood ankle deep in the shocking brightness of green paddy, planting rice. He would continue reciting the poem until he came to the last lines or encountered a stray cow in the road – whichever came sooner – as he could rarely remember how it ended, his voice trailing off and getting lost in the blare of traffic. And now, as he sat in his cane chair and spoke of towns growing like mushrooms, I began to see the entire island shorn of its jungle vegetation, sprouting mushroom cities, as women in folded sarongs planted golden spears of corn into the damp earth.

It was a magical world of my imagination and I must admit the translation helped. It allowed me to expect the unexpected when I arrived in my new home, keep myself open to change despite the violence of the past. I adjusted quickly to life in England, greedily claiming the new seasons, spores of belonging spreading everywhere. I watched the charts on Top of the Pops, danced in discos so my body felt different when I moved. I ate scones with strawberry jam and Devonshire clotted cream and argued over the correct pronunciation of scones. Yet my father never made the adjustments that came so readily to me.

I would lead him into spice shops and stalls of the fruit he loved, so he could take in the clashing colours and smells, and he would find his way to shelves stocked with unfamiliar things. He'd peer at jars of jellied eels and stare them into strangeness. Somewhere, between the tamarind paste and whitening toothpaste, between shrivelled rambutans and blushing pears, he could be found searching for that organic connection between things, touching objects with his fingertips, feeling for the history of the coins he held in his hands.

After a few years of drifting in and out of dead-end jobs I finally arrived in this village in the Sussex Downs. I knew that my father would have approved of the place if only he could have found a sense of continuity with this land. With its flint cottages and irregular windows, its Victorian pubs of panelled walls, its sloping streets of mud-spattered Land Rovers and an eighteenth century church with its sudden spire, the village of Marshdean had grown like the mushrooms that nestled in its beech woods – organically over time. It even has a slow river that had long been interrupted in its course by a mill. You can hear the river as you climb the steps towards the post-office that stands there now. The uneven floors have been covered with a hessian carpet that scrapes your shoes. A brass bell above the door alerts the postmistress to every new arrival. The bell stills your steps as you enter cautiously into a space that is edged with the faint trace of flour. I had wiped the mud off my shoes and was listening to the water outside when Mrs Hockins looked up from her open book of stamps.

'So you are from Sri Lanka?' she smiled, glancing at the letter in my hand.

'I thought you might be,' she continued, taking my silence for assent, 'but wasn't sure. It's good you have family here now that you're so far from home. Laila hasn't been as lucky. She is also from Sri Lanka, but she is on her own.'

So there it was: a potted history of my past. I bristled at the scrutiny and, the assumption that I was lucky in some way.

'Laila is Sinhalese,' she then said carefully. 'I know that must mean something to you.'

It was difficult to bear her gaze. When everyone knows your country is at war, when every new atrocity is analysed and screened in shrieking colour into family living rooms, there really is nowhere left to hide. The heft and weight of your circumstances are measured. Your identity is fixed.

She reached for the letter that I slipped under the glass screen. It was addressed to my former teacher in Colombo, a man who regarded me as a success story. I was the young scholar who'd fulfilled his own dream of gaining a First Class degree from a British university and now had at last secured that elusive permanent job. But the small communication that Mrs Hockins held in her hand marked me as a refugee, reminding me of a history I needed to forget.

'You follow the news?' I said flatly.

'Laila does. She fills us in on all the details and works herself up sometimes. It's all very sad. I think she misses home. She's not been back for a very long time.'

'Is she –' I was about to ask if this fellow stranger, too, had been a victim of war, if Laila had been forced out of the country as I had, if she was comfortable with her ethnic appellation, ask the very questions that I myself ran away from - but stopped myself in time.

'She has been here a long time?' I began licking the stamps and sticking them down.

Mrs Hockins clucked.

'Twenty years I should think. Perhaps longer. We don't see her much now. She has difficulty getting about. But she lives just round the corner from you. No.25. You should drop in and say hello. I'm sure she'd like to talk.'

Again, the blind assumptions, the gaze that searched for scars of ethnic markings – Sinhala or Tamil? – in my face, voice, clothes. How easily the name and address of one stranger were passed on to another! The resemblance to the security forces was uncanny.

'I'm sure,' I said, turning towards the door. 'I'll post this myself.'

It didn't feel safe to leave the letter with her.

If I had known then what I know now, I would have approached Laila differently, would have taken care to step around her memories and just listened as she talked. But I was young and too absorbed in my own need for connection to recognise hers. Our first proper conversation set the pattern for those that followed until her death the following year. I spoke to her through the grid of interrogation that I had got to know so well. Laila was the one who approached me first.

'You've just arrived haven't you,' she said rather than asked, from behind a trolley bright with cans and assorted fruit. 'How do you like Marshdean?'

Her eyes glistened like papaya seeds and looked rather too directly into mine.

'It's quiet,' I muttered and introduced myself with my ethnic-neutral first name as I extended my hand. My parents had had the wisdom to call me Mark, a name that travelled well.

'I'm Laila,' she smiled. 'I had heard you'd arrived.'

Her eyes softened as she invited me to her home, a meal perhaps, some 'home cooking', she said, indicating with a jewelled hand the halibut, mangoes and condiments she had assembled on the conveyor belt. I abandoned my natural caution and accepted. I hadn't had a proper meal for weeks.

Now, sitting on her high-backed chair, with her arm on the cushioned rest and her left leg raised upon a stool, she looked at me and winked.

'Not the same as Lion Lager, but almost as good,' she said indicating my glass of Cobra beer. 'But if you get the combinations right - food, drink, music, company - it can feel like you never left home.'

I drank and murmured my approval, trying to stretch my legs across the rug without touching her foot. The restricted space gave an enforced sense of intimacy to the room. I was conscious that I was a single man, whose only distinguishing feature was a past he wished to leave behind, avoiding toe contact with a woman of middle years who had lived a life as cluttered as her home. I had been told Laila had once been married to a French engineer with whom she'd had a still-born son. She was alone now, as was I, but it seemed we had little in common except memories of a place that was being transformed by war.

I scanned a batik picture above the mantel-piece. It showed a peasant woman carrying a pitcher of water, with her hip thrust provocatively to one side. The woman's tilted form reminded me of a stone figurine on the stairwell of our former home. 'Ah, my Solitary Reaper,' my father would say as he caressed the arched back of the figure. My mother would caution me to check my steps whenever I ran upstairs to remind me to be careful not to knock the statue down. That object, too, had been consumed by flames.

Laila leaned forward and adjusted her outstretched foot. A knee brace was visible just beneath her skirt.

'What happened?' I asked with feigned lightness, when she noticed my downward glance.

'Oh, just an accident,' she shrugged. 'Accident does sound a bit ominous, doesn't it? Especially in Sri Lanka where you don't know what to believe anymore. This wasn't too serious but it was a real accident, in Colombo, entirely my fault. I was careless - stepped into an open manhole and broke my leg ten years ago. It mended badly and I have not been able to walk properly since. When were you last back?'

I was being scrutinised again, but not unkindly I felt. We were linked to a place in which accident could cover a multitude of sins.

'Some time ago,' I stayed evasive. 'What about you?'

'Oh my last trip is marked right here,' she said, patting her leg. '*That* was when I was last back. It took eight months to mend and it didn't set straight. My father was furious when they said I'd never be able to walk properly again. He'd paid a fortune for the best surgeon. You know what parents are like, so protective and all. Well, he'd paid for the best and been told I'd be fine, been assured of it while they kept me in hospital, week after week. My father trained as a doctor, you see, so he knew all the right people, but he switched to journalism as he wanted to get the news on the street. He was always writing, following up stories that took him out of town. Even at home, we'd hear him typing thup-thup, late into the night. And now he's retired, he's still writing, but it's just letters to me. Beautiful letters remembering the good times before war. And I write back of course and tell him everything, well everything there is to tell about what goes on in this place. It is strange, don't you think, living in this forgotten village when our country is in such a state and in all the newspapers. I sometimes imagine myself at home again, walking barefoot with grass under my feet, and am startled when I wake up.'

'Did your father practise in Colombo?' I asked and went on to ask all the other questions that might pin him down. His age, caste, community, family history, as if these things were the things that mattered, as if her father could be claimed like new-found territory, when in fact what mattered of course were the gaps in understanding, the silenced, secret spaces of love.

I asked all the conventional things and she answered generously, with trust. She was telling me of her father's love of clocks, especially mantle clocks, and his favourite French clock with the brass figurine of a dancer that resembled her mother. She was telling me these things as the smell of tamarind entered the room. She told me of the way her father wore his old school tie askew on his Sunday walks by the sea so it would flap like a fish about his face. She told me of his lobeless ears, a family trait he had inherited, and how on account of this he'd been called a blockhead, as a lack of lobes indicated he was definitely not another Bodhisatva, a future Buddha.

Laila's mother had died when she was born. Her father had brought her up and still rang her every day before the evening news. If it wasn't for his calls, she said, she'd not have been able to watch the Channel Four broadcasts on the war.

'He tells me not to worry and I tell him things are bad, very bad, that he's got no idea how bad, and should take care living in that town with the military breathing down his neck. It's all Muslims and the army, sudden killings every day. It's a struggle for a Sinhala journalist but he tells me it's safer with the soldiers around. But how can he know the truth with the censorship and all? How can any of us be sure what is really happening there? You know Mark,' she paused and slowly stirred her tea, 'it is only because he speaks to me like this that I feel I can carry on.'

I watched her as the smell of tamarind gave way to the tangy warmth of lemon grass.

'Enough about me,' she sighed. 'Tell me how you came to be here.' She was looking straight at me and I knew she knew – without my telling – what had prompted me to leave. It was there in every word, every gesture, in my quick-fire questions, in the scar upon my cheek.

'You came in '83?' she said softly.

Not a rhetorical question this, but an incomplete sentence, one I felt compelled to carry on. And so, despite myself, despite – or perhaps because of – all the barriers, checks, and stiff-lipped scrutiny that had clipped my history and gave me leave to remain in England, I told her, quickly and erratically, of the never-before-talked-about things as if speaking of them might spirit them away.

I told her of the night of Black July, when rumours hotter-than-fire spread through the city, of shouts that splintered our front door and the ice-in-the-belly fear. Of armed youths that I recognised from school, of knives, sticks and bottles of petroleum, of being bound fast by cables torn from walls. Of how we had all been forced on to the floor as they torched our house, floor by floor, leaving us in flames that shattered windows. Of our smuggled smoky exit with the help of neighbours, and our arrival into the grim-faced, bristle-browed formality of the Immigration Services at Heathrow.

I felt it necessary, watching Laila's bit lip, to stress that the neighbours we owed so much to were Sinhalese, as the memory of their fear came back to me as a stark reflection of our own. We'd been caught between the hate and shame of the Sinhalese, who'd never known where to put us, and were now caught between the distrust and fear of the British who wanted us out. We'd been kicked around like garbage and knew nothing except that we belonged nowhere and everywhere, were now weightless with flight. No wonder we needed Eelam, that imaginary nation that rivalled the imagined kingdom of the Sinhalese. It sounded good, I confessed. Eelam, our land. A land of our own.

I stopped as I realised I was saying things I wasn't aware of believing till now.

'Did all of you make it here? Father, mother, brother?'

'Yes.'

It had not occurred to me my family might have been separated by the war.

'And they are in London now?'

'Yes. I see them from time to time.'

'That's good. It is important, very important to be together,' she said rising and slowly making her way to the kitchen.

'And your father,' I called after her, conscious for the first time that she was an exile of sorts too. 'Does he come and visit you here?'

'He plans to come,' she said stirring the food and sampling some sauce that she had ladled onto her wrist. 'In summer perhaps, when the weather is fine. It's difficult. He's old and I'm less mobile now. But it doesn't matter,' she brightened as she made her way back to her chair. 'We talk on the phone, so in a way he's visiting all the time. All the time, any time, I just pick up the phone and he's there. And I write, tell him my thoughts, describe this place with its narrow, up-down houses. I write every day. See, here, another letter.'

She showed me a sheaf of translucent paper with tiny insect writing and I was reminded of the days my father used such paper to write to his friends abroad. The thin air-mail paper had been perfect for tracing illustrations of British wildflowers and reproducing them in my diary. Laila was showing me her letter as a testament of connection.

'Here is my latest letter. You can read it if you like.'

'No,' I was taken aback. 'But thank you.' I was not used to such trust. 'Would you like me to post it for you?' I backtracked, wanting to return the confidence in some way.

'Oh would you?' her face lit up. Even her eyes smiled. 'Thank you. It's difficult with all those steps. I cannot understand why they put the post-office on a hill. Now come-come, sit-sit,' she said pointing to the dining-table. 'That fish must be cooked now.'

From then on, I would stop by Laila's house every Friday on my way back from the station and pick up her letter to take to the post office. This small act did much to improve my credibility in Marshdean. I was no longer just an asylum seeker or an anonymous commuter, but a responsible citizen who could be relied upon. My young neighbour asked to borrow my motorbike. The publicans who lived up the High Street asked me for advice on computer software. Motorists would even stop to ask me for directions through the village. To be asked for directions was a sure sign that I belonged.

Then things got busier at work and I could not visit Laila every week. I went when I could and would sometimes hear her talking on the phone as I approached her home. Her voice would lift with laughter as she told her father off for being incapable of calculating the time difference between their two countries despite having all those clocks. She sounded so happy I did not wish to interrupt, and I never thought of inviting her to my sparse flat. She would have furnished it in her head if given half a chance.

My world expanded. I found the need to restrict my visits to Ealing to the first Sunday of every month. I continued to steer my ailing father through a jamboree of jam jars that he now accepted he would never be able to decode, and returned to work and my life in Marshdean. Business meetings, my sparse flat clear of memories and Laila's laughter behind the curtains of her home. I never confided in her again as I did on that first visit, never told her that I was due to return to the country soon. She knew my demons. What more was there to know? And I did not ask her of her life. What need was there when I carried in my pocket the vital link to her past.

Her letters were always unsealed, a fact that made me feel we shared a secret pact. I never bothered to mention it to her. Why should I? I knew I would not betray her trust. I would just lick the envelope closed and hand it to Mrs Hockins who enjoyed guessing the weight before putting them on the scales.

'I thought so. That'll be one pound ninety-six,' she smiled. 'Laila must have had a lot to tell her father this week.'

And Laila's letters had indeed been getting heavier so it was getting difficult to seal them. I began to wonder what she could be writing about, what on earth she could be doing to fill all those pages with words.

One Saturday I left home later than usual and found the post office doors locked. I returned to my flat with her letter in my hand and put it on top of the TV to remind myself to post it when I next went out. That night as I turned the TV off, my hand brushed open the envelope which, as always, had been left unsealed. It was then that I gave into a temptation I did not know I had and drew out the wad of pages and began to read.

It was a wild, whooping letter, full of intimate details of a life that her father would never see. A letter sweet with the taste of the wild turnips that had erupted in her garden, warm as the mint tea with a hint of ginger (which she would make when he came to see her!) that brought feeling back to her cold toes, noisy as the drilling from the new road works that set her teeth on edge. It was as haphazard as the butcher's gossip, unexpected as the delivery of Mrs Fletcher – the newsagent's – new grandchild, subtle as the milky sunsets that blurred the distant hills into oneness and made her wish he were there so they could share the same sky.

The letter then slid into a sudden anxiety and became wracked with an anguish that registered all the things we dared not discuss. Abductions, killings, disappearances (of twelve children!) in the East, the possibility of Tiger conscriptions and the silencing of the press, pleas that he should stay in Colombo and not – on any account - return home. Laila told him that he shouldn't give anyone details of his whereabouts or movements, reveal that his diabetes had got worse – even this might be used against him if neighbours turn him in; and dear Father, she had one special favour to ask of him, but only if he could ensure it was safe to carry it out. She knew he was careful and she wondered if he might, just this once (what with all his contacts) find out something that would really help a friend of hers. She was worried about Mark, the Tamil lad who had lost his home – her father will remember her mentioning him. Or more precisely, she was worried about Mark's father, who by all accounts seemed to be losing his mind. Dear Father would know all about the psychological impact of their loss. Mark's father seemed to have paid a heavy price – not only lost his home but all sense of who he was. Mark did not say much but she could tell what was happening from the look in his eyes. His father was suffering and it would really help if he could be told what had become of his former home.

Whatever happens, dear Father, you mustn't put yourself at risk, but if there were any way – and I don't want to ask but must – might it be possible for you to make some inquiries about their case? It would make such a difference to these people. Mark is a dear, kind boy, without him I would not be able to write to you like this. His family have lost everything. We must help them if we can. Here is the address - If you could do this, dear Father, without taking risks …

I read the letter again and again, reading into a morning that became a blur. I woke that Sunday to be told by my moped-borrowing neighbour that Laila had died in her sleep of a stroke. Her death came without warning. My sense of order and of time seemed to break with the news. Just a few days later I found myself on a plane bound for Colombo with Laila's unsealed letter zipped into the pocket of my case.

The day after my arrival in the city I stepped down from a taxi before a block of flats. I walked to the security booth and said I had come to see Laila's father. The guard paused and scrutinised my facial scar, my silk tie, checking out the Tamil expatriate. He buzzed and spoke into the intercom, saying something in Sinhala that I could not understand.

'Upstairs,' he said in English. 'Second floor.'

I walked up and stepped into Laila's Sri Lankan life and there, on a couch by the front door, was a stack of envelopes addressed in her tiny script.

'I have been waiting for you,' the old man said. 'I would ask you to sit down but as you see there is no room.'

'I am very sorry for your loss,' I shook his hand. 'Laila was my friend. This is her last letter. She wrote so many. I had not realised.'

He put out a hand to decline the letter. 'Yes, but all unread as you can see.'

I wanted to laugh. This was some joke, surely – an old man's twisted sense of humour. But he smiled and shook his head.

'I am not Laila's father,' he said, leading me into a dark room that contained a bed. 'He lived here. I was his friend. He was a brave, stubborn, bloody-minded man. I knew it would end badly but Laila kept writing even though I told her to stop.'

I found myself leaning against a cabinet to steady myself as the old man went on to tell me of his friend's last days. How the indomitable journalist had been investigating a case of a missing youth – a complicated case involving corruption at the highest level – it was best not to say more. How the inevitable death threats took many forms, but the more intense the harassment, the more relentless his friend's pursuit of facts. How that final day a call had come that had excited the old writer – he'd been given news, he said, that would clinch the case. He'd begged his friend not to leave, but he'd insisted, and driven off into a darkness that had taken over the flat. Laila had not listened when he told her that her father had disappeared.

'She insisted I was lying, that if she could still hear his voice then he must be alive. The poor child was deluded and would keep writing to him every week. I know my friend is lost, but I keep all these letters just in case Laila's right. When there is a disappearance and no body, you hope and keep hoping. Hope is what keeps us alive don't you think?'

The old man looked at me in a way that reached out and spoke to my deepest self. In that instant, I felt stronger and knew what I had to do. I knew at once that this last letter, which could never be delivered, still carried a hope that might be fulfilled. That Laila's hope for her lost father might lead me to help mine.

I did what was necessary, was as efficient as required, and went straight from Heathrow to the house in Ealing on my return. Within minutes I had thrust the photograph that Laila's father might have taken, if he'd had a chance, into my own father's hand. It showed a new, colonnaded house, fronted by a manicured lawn, in the space where our rambling house had once stood. Our ancestral home, which had been extended over the years, was gone; only the wrought iron front-gate was still there. Our home was gone and needed to be imagined from what remained. I had completed the task Laila had set her father and found our former home.

The TV anchorman was reporting on a fresh conflict in

another part of the world as my father adjusted his glasses and bent down to look at the photograph in my hand. He squinted at the high roof, the majestic columns and the carved wooden doors framed by potted palms. I showed him the iron gate and the old road sign to assure him it was indeed where we once lived, that things had moved on, that the damage could not be undone. But it was useless, he wasn't listening, just kept peering at the photo as if he did not know what it was.

I began to regret my foolishness - how absurd to assume I could single-handedly unravel the transformations of time! - when he drew back and held up a trembling hand, pointing at an image in the photo under the porch of the new house.

'Son, look here,' he exclaimed. 'See. Can you see it there!'

And I saw – just as he did – something I had missed in my haste to get the picture, to get away from that place.

'Those bastards have taste!' my father shouted. 'Look, there it is. Come call your mother. This is big news. This she must see!'

For the first time we sat together on the sofa, oblivious to the news reports, as he began reciting the old poem from our long car journeys, moving steadily on. The words came streaming from him as he laughed and plucked the picture from my hand, this picture that showed a new house, a stranger's porch and there – in a clear band of sunlight – our statue of the solitary reaper that I would brush past on my return from school.

Yes, there it was standing by someone else's front door, calling us back, carrying my father on a journey that took him to those last forgotten lines. *The music in my heart I bore*, he cried out, flinging his arm about my mother, *Long after it was heard no more.*

Completing the verse. Restoring the end.

Kethumathie

My mother grew up in Kethumathie, a house called Heaven. A house with rooms so large you could slip another home into them, ceilings tall enough to swallow secrets, floors so broad they urged walkers into waltz. The dining room alone could accommodate three hundred people. Men lived in the right wing and women in the left. There were discrete bachelor quarters for unmarried sons. It was a grand, beautiful, lonely place.

My grandmother hated living there as she hated not being mistress of her own home. She hated the laugh of her mad sister-in-law who was locked away for her own good. I can see my mother, as a child, peering from a chink by the heavy jakwood doors at her grandmother as she bends over her desk, filling in the accounts for the day. When the old lady dies there is no diary, just books of names and numbers. My own grandmother, my mother's mother, is seated at an ebony dressing-table, watching herself in triplicate. The mirrors talk to her as she puts rubies to her ears. It is eight in the evening.

At eight o'clock, the newspapers report that Dr Emanuel from Kethumathie Hospital arrived home after work. He is a careful man with precise fingers. Inserts the key in the door and turns it smoothly. His wife looks up from her desk and smiles.

To find Kethumathie you need to either know where it is or look hard, for the country has few landmarks. You turn left off the main road in Panadura not far from the timber yard and follow the red road for about 150 metres. It is a road like any other, broken and grassy. On your right you come upon a high white wall and, if you follow this wall round a corner, you will come to a large wrought iron gate, which has been propped open. Beyond lies an arced driveway and a circular lawn with a pedestal fountain in the centre. Further back a tall white, wedding-cake of a house with filigreed eaves, long balconies and wide wings. The house is flanked by chalets that look over the lawn. Above the house, there is a black sign with white letters: P.C.H. Dias Memorial Hospital for Women, though people still call it Kethumathie.

You are free to enter but something about the long drive to the darkened porch and the numerous squinting slatted windows holds you back. The house defies entry. It is still a private place where women learn silence. When my grandmother gave birth to her first daughter here, the heavy doors shut out the conjoined cry of mother and child.

I see a man in blue trousers slide past me and walk onward in a hurry. I lower my head and follow his quick steps, seeking anonymity. I am aware of his polished shoes crushing the gravel and my own ill-fitting sandals. We climb the steps and are in. The receptionist does not see me as I enter the vast hallway. There is a long stairway ahead that splits into two and disappears into darkness and four or five open doorways where tall curtains sway. He is gone. He could be anywhere and I am lost.

This is a country without landmarks. To live here you need to make your own way across and between stories, or die without a history. Let me lead you to connection, a small moment of understanding.

I look above the stairway and see grey portraits on the walls that grow eyes, flesh and hair. My great-grandfather and great-grandmother are looking down on me. They summon me upstairs and I see them more clearly with each step. When I am half-way up, their gaze has shifted so they look beyond me and I am forced to take the last steps on my own. I am on a landing of wide steps that skewers the bowels of the house. I follow my footsteps and am in a room lined with metal beds that disappear towards the bright light of high windows.

Dinner was served at eight fifteen. The butler struck a gong and the family sat down to engraved silverware and cut glass finger bowls. My grandmother never saw the gong that regulated her day.

The doctor washes his hands under the tap, looping his palms about one another as water splashes on his chest. He turns the tap off with the pads of two fingers, shakes his hands above the sink and reaches for the hand towel. It is now eight fifteen.

I walk past the beds, touching the metal bedposts to be certain I am here. I wonder what this room was like when my grandmother lived here and try to furnish it with my eyes. But it is a room full of women, swollen women with slow, swollen eyes. They have the glass gaze of my ancestors whose portraits steady the stairwell. The dead and living draw together, along with those waiting to be born.

I move past an attendant who carries a tray of bottles and slide a bedside trolley towards her as she puts them down. She does not acknowledge me, just twists the cap off and fills a glass. A woman raises herself on one elbow, her hair unravelling behind her. When she lifts the glass to her lips and swallows, I see my grandmother's throat ripple with wine.

I hear the clink of glass and walk past the beds towards the gap where the door should be. In the past, each room was sealed by thick doors, now some are missing. The curtains across the empty doorframes breathe like sleeping women.

When I reach the banister, I look down the sweep of stairs.

Did someone laugh or cry? Something rattles and the noise seems to come from the left on the floor below. A door slams and it takes me a few minutes to reach the lowest step. These stairs have been built for slow, grand entrances, not flight.

Through the open front doors, the same man in blue trousers can be seen pacing up the drive. Some nurses are on the long veranda, murmuring as they watch him leave.

A creature cries. It is a baby. A door opens and releases a chorus of cries, all as indignant as the first. My grandmother pauses, a spoon poised to her lips. Her daughter is crying in a room upstairs. She can hear it despite the solid doors. It is a shrill, jagged cry that she wants to quash. She opens her mouth for beef curry and grinds the sound out of her ears.

At nine o'clock the doctor has slipped into a sarong and is watching the news. He absorbs it all, is capable of seeing connections where others cannot. The abduction of a youth leader; the peons' strike; the murder of a cricket coach; the death of a monk; the bribery of a cabinet minister; flooding in the north. There are two medical reports. One on the shortage of ambulances and another on the need for kidney specialists.
He remembers how his wife, a fellow doctor, had pleaded with him that they might leave for Australia. His wife is in the bedroom reading. He knows this even though he does not see her.

My grandmother speaks to the ayah. Her voice is clipped as if each word has been scissored from a sentence. She goes to the drawing room where the women are sipping news with sherry. Her sari rustles as she sits in her allotted chair. She touches the jewellery at her ear lobes and neck and is reassured.

Subramaniam is clearing the dishes when he hears someone at the door. There are more patients outside for Dr Emanuel. The doctor tells him that he will see them at the dispensary which adjoins his house and goes to collect the keys. His wife looks up from her book. She offers to see them herself as she has not changed for bed yet but he tells her that they had asked specifically for him. They hold each other's gaze, connected by this new uncertainty, but reach an understanding in silence. He turns and walks out, closing the door firmly behind.

My great-grandmother is discussing the newly-hired cook who has just been sacked. She was an assistant and the senior cook had complained that she was forgetful and clumsy. My great-grandmother had been reluctant to fire her but it was necessary to maintain harmony in her household so the girl had left that morning. My grandmother sits silent and beautiful. Domestic matters bore her and she has no say in these household affairs.

It is ten o'clock in the evening. There are five patients in all, one of whom he recognises. She is a recently discharged mother from Kethumathie Hospital who holds her baby in her arms. Behind her stand four unknown men whose bicycles are propped outside. The doctor assumes that some of the men have accompanied the woman and child on account of the lateness of hour. He leads the woman in first.
The infant has a high temperature and dry cough. He fills in a prescription and opens the cabinet for a small bottle. He tells the mother she will need to go to the pharmacy for the cough mixture in the morning but she should not worry as the baby's temperature will soon drop. The mother smiles and thanks him. She wants to tell him that the baby will not suckle since he developed the cough. The doctor notes her

hesitation, recognises it, and tells her that the baby will start
to feed normally once the fever ends. As she leaves two men
enter and tell him not to stand up.

My grandmother wants to go to bed but she knows she must
not leave the room before her mother-in-law who is now
discussing the new land laws in the east. My grandmother
remembers her last trip to Tangalle, the livid sunsets and
parties by the beach. Her eyes begin to close in sleep and red
dreams.

He knows they mean to hurt him.
'Do you remember Malithi Alwis? Hmm?'
They reach forward, past the desk, and pin his arms behind
him as he struggles to stand. A shout escapes him that seems
to come from someone else. The knife is near his face. There
is a sharp blow to his neck.
'The infant died. Her husband came to see you.'
And in an instant he remembers the distraught and angry
man in blue trousers whose eyes were red as blood. One arm
is free and he grabs a chair and thrashes. He staggers. The
door opens and the men disappear.

His wife saw the bicycles disappear with Subramaniam in
pursuit. She entered the dispensary to find her husband lying
in a red pool. His eyes were choking. She is with him now.
He knows her touch.

My grandmother strokes the rubies by her neck and adjusts
them absently.

He is lifted and carried into a van, the voices merging with
the engine's sputter. His wife holds his head, neck, shoulders,
pressing words into his ears as if to staunch the blood. He

is taken to another hospital, but in his delirium he sees the pale tapering eaves of Kethumathie, a stone slab of porch and tall ceilings that have sprung into brightness at his entry. His wife's words echo, echo and overlap. He does not know what she is saying but is aware of a gushing in his ears. He feels for her face in the brightness. Nurses appear and slide across his vision like moths. Where is she? He is reaching but cannot see her. He feels himself slip into a new space.

And there is a cry. A thin seam of sound, clear and sharp, that we all hear.

My grandmother opens her eyes. The heavy doors judder and break, casting a streak of light across her face. The nurses hear it too and look at the doctor's wife, as she cradles him and calls to him through the spreading blood. The noise swells as she reaches for her husband's face, puts her lips to his cheek and sees his mouth open large. She is willing him to speak, to voice rage, revenge, bloodlust, to call out in defiance and accommodate a sound that expands and unfurls. It sweeps along the wide, echoing walls of Kethumathie like the shriek of a new-born child.

Ventriloquy and Other Acts

Act 1: Heart

I was born in a house screened by golden bamboo that touched the sky - the spirits of light and wind and rain playing on a flute of bamboo reeds. On one side, the gentle road with its music of indolent buffalo hooves and crisp bicycle bells. On the other, the manicured lawn of blue grass curled by a sickle drive and paths fringed with croton, lobster claws, canna lilies and dwarf thambili. To the right, a gnarled frangipani tree, its twisting branches a perfect jigsaw of light and bark, tipped with an aureole of yellow flowers. The flowers would fall, spinning through the air with their stalks upright and land, petals first, like ballerinas in wide dresses, before the gardener would gather them into line with his rasping broom. The tree had grown from a sapling cut from its ancestor in my great-grandmother's garden on the south coast. Although the bamboo, lawn, original house and gardens are all gone now, both these trees still exist. Real family trees. All secrets and knowledge.

My favourite haunts were the two paved gardens on each side of the house, one of which in later years I would grandly call the Pineapple Garden because of the pineapple plant growing in the central dais. I would also find refuge in the cool arc of darkness underneath the sweeping stairs indoors where I hid my cricket bat. As children we have a more intimate sense of space and our first homes are remembered through recesses, gaps, close corners and cool floors - the shadows under the largest leaves curled into a conical nest by the tailor bird, the tunnels of wilderness beneath hanging vines that draped the house like a green fringe, the indented pattern of tiles in the drawing room whose paths I can trace with my fingertip to this day. This is how we remember. Through small certainties of touch, through patterns of enclosure.

Someone is going up the stairs, barefoot, so it is not a footfall I hear, but the clatter of a bucket and broom. It is someone whose name I once knew but who now remains nameless. One of the many who taught me my first words, my first songs, which flowers tasted sweet, which plants were not for tasting, the right grain for birds, the language of the seasons. Someone nameless taught me the first verse of the Lankan national anthem which is still all I know of it. I sing along and remember her. Nameless but not forgotten. The closest connections are often anonymous. The identity of love.

There is a tinselly tinkle of metal. It is grandmother. The overseer who walks with an armoury of keys drawn in a bunch around her waist by a silver chain so she can be heard from a distance. She has a strong voice which is high and fluting when she is chatting to friends, but which turns grainy when she is talking to those who cook, clean, serve, polish, wash, sew, iron, drive and tend the garden. (I now realise I come from a long line of ventriloquists.) There are nine servants in this house. And there are as many again in the other houses. It is a big family. And I an extra. Well-looked after, spoilt even, but in the list of domestic duties focused on the maintenance of a beautiful home and a full social calendar, an extra nevertheless. What is the value of a child in a house full of ebony antiques, jewelled heirlooms and soirées under chandeliers and European figurines? I have now found out that it is the price of food, clothes, ayahs, washing, sewing, toys, cleaning the stairway walls of my fingerprints, ballet lessons and the occasional medical bill - all itemised and mailed, unbeknown to me, to my parents abroad.

Yet the freedom of such displacement is not to be underestimated. I was, as far as I was concerned, an only child with a couple of imaginary siblings for company. These siblings had no correspondence to the real brother and sister who were living with my parents in another country and whom I had no clear memory of at all; rather they changed shape and form at my bidding and were called up when I felt the need for alternatives, an alternative world, an alternative family. This imaginary home of which I was in control. I even had an imaginary mother. She was called Pinthuré Amma, picture mother, and would appear every time her photograph was brought out: a beautiful woman with bright eyes, jewels about her neck and black curls tumbling about her face. She was a princess. *There, your mother, your picture mother.* The wonder of the imagination rests in its sanctioned infidelities, in the way it allows us to choose our lovers.

I had real lovers too. There was one person who loomed large in my life, who knew where to find me at teatime but also knew if it was wise to leave me alone, who knew with the sixth sense of true kinship if I was sad and would clap his hands, scoop me up and throw me into the air to make me squeal and forget myself - much as my own father would, years later. He was, I thought, tall, and in my monochromatic memory of him, always wore white or cream. White shirt, trousers or sarong, the latter held up by a wide leather belt. He had a sheaf of walking sticks all slightly taller than I was, and on my many walks with him I would hold silent conversations with each stick, keeping time with its pace, and getting to know its individual mood.

He was my grandfather, Seeya. My imaginary mother's father. A fairy-tale presence who bought me choc-ices and balloons at Galle Face, holding them patiently while I was lifted on for a pony-ride first, and finally when I returned home, watched me dance on the blue grass with my pink plastic cricket bat. Any intention of making me the first female national cricketer had been abandoned once my passion for dance had been discovered by my mother's older sister who had been told that ballet lessons would help strengthen my fallen arches. I would skip, pirouette and polka hop my way around the lawn or on the parquet reception hall, with feet that remained as flat as a duck's.

My memories of my first years are bound to this house and these people. I know that certain facts can be questioned. Was the blue grass planted later? Did Seeya ever wear white? - but my earliest memories, my first birth, will always belong to this place where I grew up, far from the land where I was in fact born. Those of us who inherit multiple time zones require such false memories to tell us who we are. Our belonging is mediated not by the truth of fact but by the truth of experience. And so Aruna, this house called dawn, built by my grandfather shortly after Independence, has become my birthplace and my mother has become an imaginary apsara. Mine was an immaculate birth.

My grandmother has finished giving instructions to someone whose name I once knew but cannot remember, and retires to her bedroom, jingling, for her massage. I have seen what goes on there and still wonder at the practice. The masseuse a thin, dark woman kneading my grandmother's warm, buttery flesh into round rolls, down, down, and then cupping small sections and popping them into animation. The masseuse getting thinner and my grandmother expanding by the minute.

I hear the spray of water on leaves, leaves on water, and creep out from under the stairs, tiptoe across the dining room, and squeeze through an open French window towards the other paved garden - the one with the stone spiral staircase rising to the balcony of crimson bougainvillea. It is possible to slip from under the stone stairs, follow the curve of the annexe, and pass, unnoticed, into the tunnel of plants growing under the hanging vines. I know he will be here - the nameless gardener whose bare feet peep out from under the vines. I can smell the earth, the plants, the cool, green smell of vegetation. I have an earthworm's knowledge of such things and can tell you that these odours are headiest in the waterfalls near Bandarawela, where the raw rock, mountain water, and smell of wet moss, fern and tea-rooted earth meet. The family holiday home there is called Suramma and years later it will be sold, a village springing up bearing its name. There are other legacies, ancestors with buildings and roads named after them, whose statues now provide a perch for weary seabirds. I do not know how to relate to such myths - the cementing of private past into public history. I am only sure of the certainty of water on stone, water on moss and this wild, green smell of greedy earth. The senses are eternal; the senses are transient. The stone becomes a stone when it is touched.

Above me they are beating the mattresses on the balcony. Flat panes of sunlight smashing onto striped sausages of bedding. An ayah, is it Margaret? (who gave me lice, so that my evenings were spent on an aunt's lap as she combed and re-combed my hair as I watched the rain fall into cool wells from the corrugated roof near the vegetable patch at the back of the house) is talking to a housemaid who is doing the beating. She knows where I am of course. She always does. But she cannot see me, so I remain unclaimed, untouched. *Noli me tangere. Noli me* - my name inverted, Latinised. I was meant to be alone.

Birds are calling, painting the sky with their cries. The ring of a bicycle bell and another call, *Malu, malu, malu.* It is the fish-seller. Ayah claps her hands and calls him over from the balcony. The gatekeeper draws the latch and pulls the gate open just wide enough to let him in on his bike. Cook comes round, wiping her hands on her apron, and asks if there is a good chunk of thora in his pannier. I can hear her voice in Sinhala but the words come to me in English. Is this where memories disappear? Into the space between words, between time zones? And how can I get those first words back? Those original words that are tumbling out of Cook's mouth as she tells him to hurry as she has left the dhal on the stove. My first language was Sinhala. It was the only language I knew in those days. And these memories are a crude translation into a language I learnt later but which now possesses me. Is the gap between reception and repetition always unbridgeable? Is the listener no longer the speaker? Have I lost an inheritance or is my inheritance a loss? I do not know. I am only telling you what it is like to remember these things, to relive them now that we are trying to make sense of a different time in which language and memory are contested and revised. My purpose is recuperative. Recuperate. To recover, to find sustenance.

The fish seller has followed Cook to the pantry at the back, his bicycle wheels sliced into a segment of spinning spokes by the hanging vines. The pannier has been opened and the rich smell of blood quickens the senses. The supple rhythms of the sea have affected Cook's tongue and she is now haggling like a fish slipping between water plants. She is an excellent haggler. Not because she knows the current price of goods but because she can detect human resistance by subtleties of gesture, inflections of tone, finding in the quiver of an eye or syllable that flash of hesitation required to topple the whole process into a downright bargain. The finest thora at half the market price. Cook gives the sternest of smiles and then softens, inquiring about the fish seller's wife.

There have been many others. The breadman, the fruit seller, the coconut vendor, the knife sharpener, the kerosene man, even the broom-merchant who briskly bangs his metal cart every three paces as he walks on a road swept by bamboo shadows - all are victims to Cook's sixth sense. The quiver of an eye or syllable. The days of intimate battle.

I am getting thirsty. The plants have darkened with water. A green tailor-bird settles by a leaf, taps its tail in sharp scissor cuts and flies off.

'Small madam will get wet if she stays there.'

I am exposed. I hurry back to the patio breaking a leaf on the way.

My brother, the mythical one who lives abroad, had once built a fortress of sand by the ground here, and scraping amongst the leaves and gravel I have found the rounded remains of bastions, a vestigial stick ladder and two small soldiers. An unfinished game of an unseen sibling that, many monsoons later, I pick up, finding form and pattern in the fragments. Children are natural explorers perhaps because of such connections in the history of play, the history of imagination, and because history itself is an imaginative act. A doll from Mesopotamia, a doll from Mexico. The rituals remain the same.

White shapes are gathering in the dining room. Moths among silver. The table is being laid. Embroidered napkins, dishes of gold-plated scrollwork - all with my grandfather's initials curled snugly into amber and blue filigree so that flowers spring from his name, crystal finger bowls, a carafe with its lace cover fringed with coloured beads (so that to this day I swallow the sound of beads on glass with every drink of water), the elegant silver bell that will rest by my grandfather's right hand when he wants to summon someone, and warm, fragrant ovals of rice, curry, mallung and sambol. The fan is turned on, sending chips of light spinning across the glassware. David, the houseboy, reaches for the metal gong that is cupped between the palms of two small elephant tusks, and makes it sound just once. Slippers shuffle into life and there is movement on the stairs. I cut past like an arrow and head towards the breakfast room. Until I am tall enough to sit at the dining table, I will eat here. Away from the solemnity of silver and the danger of broken family plates.

My mother, the imaginary one who will later reclaim me,

is able - like all those whose personal knowledge is thinned to fine slices of time - to pare me down to two defining characteristics. I was, she says, a quiet child and a difficult feeder. I would sit before food as at a funeral, watching a fresh meal stiffen into a corpse. Soft, warm puffs of rice would harden into cold lumps, slices of succulent fish curl into dry leaves, pappadum absorb the texture of the season, and the hands of the breakfast room clock make several revolutions before I ate a few grudging mouthfuls.

'If you haven't finished your food by the time *that* hand of the clock has moved here, I will use *this*.'

The only time my father threatened me with the cane.

The ayahs resort to more subtle measures: tickling my chin (I would often nod off to sleep at the table), and whooping *Kakkah enava, kakkah enava* to get me to look up at an imaginary crow in the hope that my lips would part and allow a spoon in. Each mouthful an orchestrated surprise. The indolence of an empty stomach.

Lunch could take three hours. Mealtimes would sometimes blur to the point where a day felt like one long spell at the table with short breaks in between. It was thought boarding-school would cure me, but all it did was teach me new tricks of deception.

Perhaps this is why my unseen mother left me here in Aruna, because I rejected her appetite for controlled care. After watching me lose weight, she had resorted, upon a doctor's advice, to using a pipette - an ugly contraption of glass and rubber with a long cord. My lips would be prised apart and the tube inserted, regardless of whether I was awake or not. She knew I wasn't sucking when milk starting leaking from my mouth. She kept the pipette and gave it to me after I got married. *Here, our first battle.*

The breakfast room is functional and mutates over the years, taking on the colour of family needs. Today it has just a square table, a few scattered chairs and stray toys; much later it will be a restroom where my grandmother will listen to a walnut wireless pouring out the melodies of the late Jim Reeves - a liminal space where she can close her eyes, listen to songs of desire and longing while, at the same time, being conscious of the rice being pounded in the square outside. Romance and ground rice. Even later it will be my private study where tutors will teach me English, French and Maths. Mrs Oorloff, who used Lear's verse to transform sparrows into spicy birds, and an unnamed septuagenarian who placed maths books on the table, set me work, then unfolded his newspaper and proceeded to read it while he took the occasional pinch of snuff to his nostrils, algebra remaining a sniffy affair for the rest of my days.

And decades on, this room will reverberate to the massive blast of a bomb in an ancient war of belonging.

It is an ordinary room, not meant for public view. It is probably unchanged a year from now when my grandfather is having breakfast here. He coughs and collapses. David carries him to his bed where he lies unconscious for hours. Priests in saffron robes gather about him and chant pirith, their voices moths in moonlight. Seeya slips into the permanence of a sky without stars, a smile upon his lips. When they lift him from his bed they find a tiny photograph of a child under his pillow. An image of me. His last dream perhaps; my first loss. 'I will die of a broken heart', Seeya said when I left, and, of course, he did. Love can make casual killers of us all.

The afternoon is a time for repose, for birdsong and quiet roads. Adults retire to their bedrooms, strip down, turn on ceiling fans and drop off to sleep under cool strokes of air.

I am taken to bed with a small bar of chocolate and watch the mosquito net bobbing like a parachute above me. The breath of the fan, a bicycle bell, spirals of birdsong entwining and spinning apart. Sounds to dream by. You can hear your heart beat.

In a dream I hear voices on the stairs, a low murmur and the sound of a distant door opening. Rene and Eunice have arrived. Rene is tiny and frail, with small uncertain spectacles and a halo of curls. Eunice is solid and stout and has an angry mass of hair that does battle with a silver grip at her neck. I loved one and was terrified of the other. Had to pass one to get to the other.

I slip out of bed, clutching the melting Kandos bar in my hand. Eunice has positioned herself in front of the sewing machine and is pressing the pedal in erratic pulses, her back turned to me so I remain unnoticed. Rene is sitting on the step by the door to the porch balcony, turning the cloth towards the light, drawing, with each stitch, a fine thread of light into the house. She does the darning. She is the gentlest person in the world.

'Here Rene,' I say, pressing the bar against her palm and stilling it.

'Why thank you child, ' and a smile to light a candle by.

How was I to know that miles away from here, years away from now, she was to die of such misplaced care?

'Rene died,' my mother said.

'Of what?' I asked.

'Probably of starvation.'

My mother had travelled a distance to carry a jar of Marmite to Rene's door at a time when she was too weak to get up and open it. Food was rationed then.

Marmite and chocolate for one who wove love into our home.

And how to connect this to my pleasure at feeding birds? Every day my grandmother would open the parlour door and place a metal cup in my hands. I would be allowed one measure of rice from one of the huge jute sacks that lay fattening on the floor, a sharp block of sunlight slicing the air into a fury of flour dust. One level cup of rice. I would scatter the grains like confetti and watch the sparrows gather.

In the evenings a shadow carries incense to each corner, tracing the contours of the house with smoke to keep mosquitoes at bay. I am left with a map of incense and recesses, of unknown footfalls and sudden stars.

The rhythm of this house still plays in my pulse, as my fingers tap the keys before me; this slow surrender of the being I call myself to a melody that will live on long after I and those about me have gone. I set these things down as a sunbird catches a tune from the frangipani leaves and releases it to music in its cry.

I left Aruna when I was four years old and began a new life in a new country with a new family, the substantial world of romance gone forever. As we get older reality hardens and seeks to deny us the truth of our imagined selves. My grandfather knew this. 'I will die of a broken heart', he had said, and, of course, he did.

The day of his funeral was my first day at school. My father drove me to school. My mother stayed at home, drawing her memories like a shawl about her. Grief is a divisive act, our memories are ours alone.

We go our separate ways, following the path of our separate sorrows.

Act 2: Funicular Relations

There is no road from Colombo to Kuala Lumpur. No direct line. You can travel by air or on water. Shifting currents. I now spend my nights between the parentheses of my parents' bodies to help me adjust to my new life. These strangers who call me theirs.

'You arrived in a short dress with pink bows and just stood there. I said "You go to her" and your father said "No, no, you go." Eventually I went and picked you up and kissed you and you were fine. You knew who we were. They had prepared you well.'

ଞ

257 Ampang Road is a solid address, time-defying, but I can barely remember the place, just a large lawn and three visual scraps.

In the first, I show my stamp album to the neighbour's Alsation by a covered passageway. A bland picture signifying nothing.

The second shows a small storeroom where a bee buzzes by the ceiling. I am certain I will be stung. A whirr of wings, a spark of pain, and voices enlarging as my cheek swells.

The third is in bold technicolour. No mere picture, this image releases my first real trace of fear. I am woken at night by the sound of running water and make my way to the bathroom where my mother lies still on the floor, her whole body darkened by water, her eyes closed, and her blue floral dressing-gown gathered by a belt about her waist. She is lying in a pool of liquid while my father stands by the bath, filling a bucket and then pouring its contents upon her, her small face and body splattered by shards. The bathroom floor is glossy, too bright for shadows. My brother and sister stand behind me. My father is shouting at us, above the gashing water, to go away, back to bed, and somehow his white anger freezes into a certainty that he is hurting her, killing her, and that we have caught him in the act.

I did not know then that my mother was prone to fainting. I did not know then that my father knew no better way of bringing her round. Such tragi-comic misconceptions reveal small fears, small truths.

I keep a diary. The entry reads: 'Nothing happened today.' The entry reads: 'Amma and Thatha quarrelled.' Over and over, the mantra of empty days and dissolution.

ಬಿ

Another land, another border, and our first home is the President Hotel in Hat Yai. For almost a year a dining table is cleared after breakfast and I am taught English and Maths by my mother. She is an excellent teacher. Pencils, paper and sugar-lump numeracy.

My brother crushes stink-bombs in the hotel lift and the changing rooms by the pool. A space-clearing act.

There are to be two more homes here, each with forbidden rooms and permitted spaces. My world has shrunk and broken. I have lived in three lands and will soon leave this fractured family space. I am six and a half years old.

These island memories are abandoned spaces I have not visited for a long time. They require a compass, a camera, and a dictionary of sorts. I hide these under my diary on my shelf at my first remembered school and hope to use them on my return.

ಣ

The approach to Uplands School begins with a funicular railway. You stand at the bottom of the hill with the other children and their parents, waiting for the cable car to reach you. All the parents and children have withdrawn into white-knuckled knots of isolation, their lips thinned to dark lines of control.

Electricity passes through them.

Occasionally someone breaks into hot white tears and the small group stirs.

You were so good. You never cried. All my children were good. I was proud of you.

And I want to make her proud.

The cable car makes a slick descent, its unseen alter ego gliding to the top of the hill. Parallel lines that give the illusion of connection.

The children scramble in and the doors click shut.

We are drawn into the jungle at an angle that is almost vertical. The ferns slide and the tall trees extend on our approach, then teeter and slip into smallness. We are drawn up into a darkness of softly falling trees and strain against the loss of foothold, feel the cables hiss and stretch, pulling something taut within us.

It will be at least six weeks before we see our parents again.

We disembark midway, the point at which the two cars draw together without contact. There is a twenty-minute walk on a road of silvery chips bordered by a bank of lolling pitcher plants so prone to landslips that the earth is constantly renewing itself. The smell of exposed roots is everywhere.

When I reach the school my first thought is how cool it is up here and how beautiful the dahlias and chrysanthemums - highland flowers that remind me of Bandarawela. After the hot bustle of motorised trishaws, street hawkers, evening bazaars with blaring pop music, sizzling satay stalls, and late nights watching my mother meticulously sewing nametapes on every vest and every sock, I am transported to a calm new world of order and control. In front there is a sharp drop and a vista of uninterrupted green, heady with unseen life. Behind me, my new home: Hillview, the infant wing of the school, where I choose a bed with a red bedspread against a window. It is in the middle of a row of beds and faces another row, all with different coloured bedspreads. I am allowed one shelf of a wooden dresser for toys and books and about six square inches on top for my hairbrush and comb. I have a diary, a sketchpad and pencils, Skipper (Barbie's sister), a packet of assams or salted plums, and some silver snap hairgrips. It is best to travel light.

Time is static. There is no boundary to loss.

They have gone. Taking my knowledge of myself with them, carrying all there is of me away in one last hug. I am now tumbling in air, without compass.

There are children draped in mist, matrons in white dresses, and a place scrubbed clean of history. I become aware of the nails curling into my palms, the thick line of dryness spreading down my throat, the hardness of the eyes that refuse to blink. There is an art to letting go.

And here are words to guide you. A prospectus of sorts.

My stay at Hillview lasts just a few weeks. During this time I sing with Miss Berenger - a fellow Sri Lankan - and take ballet lessons on Wednesday at the 'big school' where I meet my sister. I learn to dread mealtimes, squabble with Annie who borrows my doll without permission and then loses its clothes; I vomit in bed, and shit by accident on the bathroom floor. Understand the shame of it.

I am told I will be moved to the big school to a more

appropriate class. It seems that my mother's tutoring has paid off. After the move I am a year younger than my classmates and still end up coming first. My parents notice these things and I am pleased because they are.

The big school constitutes the main part of Uplands and is a mile and a half away, further up the hill. Cut proud from the jungle, the former hotel is approached by a wooden bridge on one side of which stand the dwellings of gardeners, cooks and dhobi men. Beyond lies a succession of white colonnaded buildings that have been converted into classrooms and teachers' quarters, lining a flowered path covered by a trellis draped in jade blossoms the shape of sharks' teeth.

Follow this path beyond a large encircled tree and you will find yourself at the bottom of a series of white stone steps leading to a building that rises from the landscape like a sugared villa. It has vaulted verandas and slim white pillars and looks unlike any other building I have seen before apart from, perhaps, Kethumathie. Inside there is a large dark hall with a polished wooden floor divided into a dining area and an assembly room, and on one side a library and on the other extensive kitchens. Huge wooden panels on the walls announce the winners of the Dux and other prizes in gold capitals, while neat lines of benches script the hall and punctuate the trestle tables of the dining room. It is a place that is out of time. Visitors would be forgiven for forgetting which part of the world they were in. If, however, you don't climb up here and instead choose to slip past to your left, you will gradually go down a terraced path of shallow steps, passing a sheer wall of jungle on one side and rocks as large as elephants on the other.

And I would love to leap from step to step
weightless

      elastic

         energy

drawing hungry langurs from the trees
till I reached the crest that drops down to the netball court,
playground and encircling dormitories.

From up here you are a deity.

You witness the scattered shriek and scuffle of play, the
tiny punctuation marks of matrons, the swoop of parakeets,
and the dark splash of leaves where unseen fruit bats and
flying foxes slip and slide.

Behind the dorms, which once served as holiday chalets,
lies another playground where the children are playing
Bulldog (the 'British' tag being dropped in this culturally-
sensitive country) and in the corner stands a square house
by a large rock. It is on uneven ground and one half of it
is mounted on stone stilts - as indeed, you will see, are all
the rectangular dorms if you look at them from behind. This
is the Club, housing the games rooms, TV room, informal
library and a small room containing a record-player and
rather hopefully called the disco. To your right, and on your
level, is a pretty, isolated chalet with tats drawn down. This
is Sick Bay, where Sister Chooi is on hand with gentian
violet for cut knees, milk of magnesia for constipation and
the occasional spoonful of cod liver oil. Once a term, the
nauseating smell of barley water exudes from here and we all
queue up for a nose-pinched dose.

Against Sick Bay is a path cut against living rock and musty,
secret caves that winds round and climbs back towards the
Main Hall.

Yes, there is plenty of space here. Space for concealment.

ॐ

To an outsider, the jungle is illegible. It is all riot, chaos,
a cacophony of darkness. But if, as a child, you are taken
here and then left in a sugar bowl of buildings where time

is flattened to the disc of a metal gong, where dwellings are precariously balanced upon fortified rock, where human connection is controlled by signs that forbid the glance of skin on human skin, then the dense embrace of vegetation, of rich, untranslated mothering calls, of silver movements that slither against your spine registering quick, untold life, become a scripture, a narrative of belonging, as truthful to your instincts as your lost home.

The jungle is a place of relativity. It accommodates trees taller than time and is dense with spores of longing. Here the cultures of ape, mynah bird, python and millipede clash and connect in violent harmony, assimilating those refugees amongst us who seek sanctuary in its green vaults.

The millipede pedals up the road of my arm feathering the fine hair into new legs. A trace of travel.

The jungle is generous and garrulous as monsoon rain. Prise the stone from its shell of soft moss and see it pulse in your hand. Here, touch this water into laughter. There are orchids the colour of fresh blood, lime-tongued pitcher plants with bellies bulging with sap and a translucency of wings.

There are sticky constellations of infant snails. Red ants trickling down the furrows of trees. This place transports us to another altitude, a time beyond birth and memory. If you look into a pool of water you will see nothing but pebbles.

My body is changing. There are patches on my face like sifted sunlight. A doctor calls it a fungus and prescribes an ointment. At night I feel as though a million tiny mouths are nibbling my skin. *Lichenlust*. Curling fingers into tendrils. I am reduced to flecks of haiku.

Shrinking mimosa
see these leaves of shy fingers
stroked into prayer

How to make a pot -
descend below the chalets
red earth rain water

shape into sunlight
polish with talc then paint in
the colour of joy

I wake up and find
a monkey at my window
who is the scared one?

Bucket in the bath
we queue to pour cold water
over our bodies

Forest fern of felt
fingers curling about yours -
connection and tryst

Four tall friends – Audrey,
Sophiane, Li and Michael
lines of solitude

Saturday art club -
this arm an oar in water
mirror of blue ink

Parallel lines and
duplicity of dreams - which
world do I wake to?

Your weekly letter to your parents is checked (ostensibly for spelling mistakes and grammar) and the matrons keep a diary of your bowel movements. You have ownership of one thing: your imagination.

Vigilance. Control of mind and body. This is the Buddhist ideal.

Darkness and a coruscation of pilgrim stars. You obliterate yourself in dreams. I am so good at this that I have actually started shrinking, my lips turning to parchment and my skin disintegrating to dust, so that by morning a small, shiny worm is left to slip into a groove of good conduct, sleek as amnesia.

At the end of five years I have even begun to master the art of finishing my meals on time. The mechanics are quite simple. Chew nine times and swallow with water, repeat for as long as you can, then mash what is left and mix with the gravy on your plate, allowing for the five mouthfuls that can be concealed under loosely splayed cutlery and a potato skin.

And then there is the need to find a suitable voice.

I am due to play Puck in the school performance of *A Midsummer Night's Dream*, my size and dark skin rendering me preternatural. I rehearse my lines at night, after climbing into bed, repeating them over and over, eyes bright with elfin mischief in front of an imaginary audience containing my parents. *I am Puck. Some silly humans are coming here! I'll hide and see what happens.* Cue for Bottom (alias Jimmy) to join me behind the screen and emerge with a donkey's head with eyes that roll in opposite directions.

My first performance in front of my class is an exact rendition of these illicit rehearsals in the dark. I come out with gestures that slide into jungle magic and no voice at all. I have followed the basic rule - no talking after lights out – and find I can only whisper in the dark.

PROJECT! my Speech and Drama teacher in England would write a year later in sharp letters across my notebook, *remember that your voice starts in your stomach*. I learn to throw my voice into other people's words, find pulse in the new tongue.

Yet try as you might, you cannot please everyone. Miss Sylvia Gideon, the senior matron and school ogre, has her eye on me.

She is a big, dark woman with bulging eyes, frothy hair and a voice of thunder. It is Wednesday afternoon, sheet-changing day, and I have stripped the bed and thrown a new sheet on. *Top sheet to bottom sheet, bottom sheet to wash.*

I am tucking this in, doing my neatest hospital corner, as she talks to Miss Katy. There is a pause. Miss Gideon is observing me, and I prepare myself.

'Tell me Katija,' she booms, 'why is that girl so stunted?'

Fear and rage, fear of rage.

I wish I could sprout words that would send Miss Gideon, kicking and screaming, into a parallel world where she is dragged by her hair and lashed to a stake. *'And what shall we do with the prisoner, ma'am?' Burn, burn, burn! they chant as Miss Gideon writhes, grappling with white sheets that threaten to engulf her, her eyes bulging with alarm.*

If I could have pleated time and looked forward instead of back, if I could only listen to my adult self, this time-traveller, this shape-shifter who now strides across continents in ten-league boots, how different my life might have been. But those of us who have extinguished the past to cope with the strictures of the present are denied the gift of prophecy. The irony of our imprisonment is that in order to survive we have learned to forget that a future exists.

There is another altercation some months later. Someone has asked Miss Gideon how to spell mischievous and she drops an *i*. I raise my hand and something in my manner tells her I am not impressed.

'That's enough! The problem with you, young madam, is that you are *too big for your boots*.'

And there are conflicts whose history is lost in the cartography of scars.

⁎

None of my uniforms fit me. My sister has outgrown this place and is now in a school in Singapore. I have inherited her clothes and they are far too large. The yokes drop down to my chest and the arm holes are so low slung that they reveal a large slice of white vest as if I am in a pinafore. The pockets are beyond reach and the regulation matching underpants are bloomers that would have made grandmother proud.

In addition to this, my mother has taken to co-ordinating my play clothes with curtains and sofas at home, buying the material from one place and getting the same seamstress to make everything. I now have trousers, skirts and shorts of pink and yellow checks and a dress of blue flowers that looks good on the bedroom window. The clothes are itchy and are cut to yesterday's styles. I feel like a freak when I walk about but am almost invisible when I sit down at home as I blend with my surroundings perfectly. Only my custom-made black shoes with inbuilt arches, poking out like giant army boots, give me away.

At a fancy dress party, I pin my hair into a small bun, add wrinkles and spectacles, and call myself Mrs Oldglass, a loose anagram of my name, an oddball amongst the cute kittens and cowboys.

In another land my mother writes from a house she has made into a home. We have left a rambling old place - a tropical gothic - for a house by a lake. I will remember the old place for its thrill of hidden danger. The disused swimming-pool that drew snakes to their death during the drought leaving us with a pit of twitching water, the tickling toad that lay nestling unseen in my wellington boot and sprang to life when my foot got stuck inside, and the giant cactus by the front door draped in silver stockings of snakeskin. I once found a snake here massaging her way out of her shiny sheath, flexing her length of long muscle against the cactus spines; a rasping, delicious striptease. She looked at me with cool yellow eyes and carried on as if entranced by her own vulnerability.

But I need the simplicity of the second home more. This has a garden of fruit trees - miniature orange, avocado, rambutan, mango and durian - and a warm spread of peach gladioli by the water's edge. The garden is an inheritance, but my mother adds her own touches of quiet domesticity to the house, making it a place I dare to dream about as the holidays draw near.

The living room has a cubist picture of a Malaysian market, a cane bookstand designed by my father, containing illustrated classics, a pewter vase. There are no family photos anywhere. Each time I leave for Uplands I slip pieces of folded paper about the house to be discovered after I am gone. 'Look after yourself', 'Have a wonderful day', 'Smile!', 'Sweet dreams.' By the telephone, in her hairbrush, in the fridge, under her pillow. My fingerprints everywhere. *I am here, here, here.*

I do not know my mother's inner life. After my father has gone to work, and the cook has diced the vegetables, what then?

As the term ends, we count down the days, domesticating

One man went to mow -
'Ten more days to go
ten more days of sorrow
ten more days in this old dump
and we'll be home tomorrow!'
and lapse straight into an old favourite sung to the tune of
Clementine -
'Come to Uplands, come to Uplands, it's a place of misery,
when you get there there's a signpost saying "Welcome unto
thee!"
Don't believe, don't believe it, it's a pack of flipping lies;
if it wasn't for Sir Drury, it would be a paradise.
Build a bonfire, build a bonfire, put the teachers on the top,
put the matrons in the middle and burn the flipping lot!'

This place has transformed us. We are a riot of awkward
orphans, strays, ragamuffins and rebels, with rivers of
darkness running through us.

Our parents search, their faces in the ferns.

My mother is looking at my mouth as I talk. She is convinced
that my teeth are getting out of control, that I have inherited
my father's unruly jaw and need orthodontic support. She
studies words forming and escaping as I tell her of my life,
observing the active muscle of my mouth as if it is an erratic
sewing machine. I become conscious of the chaotic connection
of lips, tongue, teeth, palate, the stumble and judder of it all.

When I close my mouth she sees me.

They have moved to yet another country.

At dawn you wake to the muezzin's cry and fold another's
prayers into your dreams.

It is my last term at Uplands and pupils in their final year have been asked to write an essay: 'What I will be doing when I am twenty-one'. I am due to join my sister at a boarding-school in England, this I know. Though at eleven years old anything is possible, my words remain pious. I write that I will look after my parents as they have looked after me, that I will live in Malaysia and may or may not marry; and then, the lines I read long after I have reached twenty-one which convince me of continuity and wholeness despite a fractured life: 'when I am twenty-one I would like to be a writer, preferably a poet, a teacher at a university or a teacher at a school'.

As I transcribe these words, dream kindles into destiny. I wrote myself a future that has now passed. Is my writing an endorsement or an erasure of time?

The white buildings rest in a jungle sleep. I have reached the end of a silver road. As I glide down the hill on these parallel lines I wonder who is coming up on the other side.

Act 3: Cold Storage

England. Land of mists, Madame Tussauds and a sulphur sun. If only I had taken my brother's renditions of Dickens to heart I might have been prepared, but everyone has kept telling me how wonderful it is, and I now have an image in my head of snow-covered skyscrapers and brilliant multiplexes full of slick shops crammed with state-of-the-art toys and revolving restaurants linked by elevated railways, an intergalactic city far cleaner and more advanced than Singapore. This image rests in uneasy equilibrium with a quieter one of women in long cloaks that have walked straight from the pages of my Classics Illustrated edition of *Jane Eyre*. I have been told that my new uniform involves this bewitching garment and am seduced into Jane's company when I try it on.

I arrive in Heathrow on a cloudy August day. I weigh as much as my baggage allowance of 44 pounds and am squeezed in the crush of Europeans who are all busy going somewhere. There is such blind white purpose here that I am convinced that a veritable wonder of civil engineering awaits me outside the airport.

My first shock comes when I get on the coach. The driver is neither Chinese nor Indian. He is European (I have yet to distinguish between British and Europeans at this stage), as European as the expatriates and tourists who ease themselves into the luxury of five-star hotels as if they were born to such comfort and who only need to emerge into sunlight to attract the custom of a dozen taxis and trishaws while the rest of us risk our lives dodging cars as we try and hail a ride home. I am just settling into my seat when the coach driver says the most extraordinary thing. *Come on up love.*

Love! He called that passenger his love! A respectable lady, twice his age, who isn't even batting an eyelid at this unwarranted familiarity. I am so unsettled by this open flirtation that I barely notice the drab uniformity of buildings that have started lengthening the roads.

Those are called terraced houses. My mother is my teacher once more. *Each door leads to a house. When I first came to England I thought the English must be very rich to own such large houses that take up a whole road.*

And for a moment I see Aruna, golden in the glow of swaying bamboo, before crushing the image into a seed as tight as my fist.

I am glad you will be in Devon, my father assured himself. *My mother was one of the first girls to gain the Cambridge Senior Certificate. She was given a copy of Westward Ho! as a prize. Westward Ho! is right by you. You will be safe. Far from London.*

How can I argue against such logic? Is my father, too, being forced, to make random connections out of the tangle of wires that make up his life, ours? What can emerge from such strange electricity?

The trip to Exeter and my sister aches to show me sheep on the hills from the speeding train. *Look there they are!* Her excitement adds brightness to the drab September day. I had expected fleecy white cuteness and instead see grains of salt, indistinguishable from the grey rain splattering the window.

I do not remember saying good-bye to my mother. She hugs a child in a smart navy suit with a cloak about her shoulders and a beret on her head.

I am not there. It is not me.

Does she, too, feel the same detachment?

ৰ০

Initiation into the brute text of England is very different from my earlier initiation into Englishness. While Englishness carried the fragrance of honeysuckle and lavender, the sizzle of candy-floss in summer and hot chestnuts in autumn and (for those of us bred on Blyton) the permanent cheer of larking about in British boarding schools, England carries no corresponding charm. It is cold, wet and blighted. Little wonder that everyone shuffles past without a word to one another, and that those who can, leave.

My priority, I discover on my first day at school, is to keep warm. This is a matter of some urgency as my skin is flaking off at an alarming rate and I have started to lose feeling in my extremities. If this carries on I will shrink and feel nothing. As clothing is restricted to school uniform for most of the day - we are only permitted to wear trousers (our warmest clothes) on Wednesday afternoons and week-ends - the only way to get warm is by having a bath. Armed with soap, towel, moisturiser and a change of clothes, I hurry to a bathroom after prep and run myself a satisfyingly steamy bath, soak there for an hour, and emerge wrinkled but warm into the dormitory. Mrs Griffin, the house-mistress, says nothing. Neither do the girls. I know that something is wrong. *You are only allowed a bath once a week. Tonight is not bath night*, whispers Sue before lights out.

I see my first robin on a yew tree by the school chaplain's house - pretty but unexceptional; watch girls illicitly smoking only to discover the warm white snake of my own breath evaporating before me; witness snow turn into sludge. These virgin sights sustain me for four seasons. Novelty is an anaesthetic to the violence of dislocation.

But this is a cycle I cannot escape. Everything is regulated. From the clothes we wear to when we wash our hair, from what we ingest to what we watch on TV; from the prising of our eyes at the wake-up bell to the sealing of our lips at lights out. We are monitored like laboratory rats.

It doesn't matter that there is no central heating in the boarding houses and that the only source of warmth is a fan at the end of corridor just warm enough to dry your hair by, it doesn't matter that there are no carpets in the dorms and that there is no hot water except in the evenings, it doesn't matter that the milk is diluted to white water and the re-constituted scrambled eggs are de-constituting on your plate, it doesn't matter that the wool blankets scratch your lungs and perforate your dreams, it doesn't matter that your canvas shoes soak through to your chilblains and your hockey stick freezes to become an extension of your arm, it doesn't matter that you are not allowed to wash your hair even if it is greasy enough to butter bread with, it doesn't matter that it takes you twenty minutes to lug your suitcase, counting *one-two-three-rest* all the way from the coach to the boarding-house while the large horsey girls you had thought were your friends stride past without lifting a finger to help, it doesn't matter that young adults are compelled to sleep on bunk beds designed for people half their age, it doesn't matter that you have to pray, sing hymns, wear abrasive uniform and walk a mile to church every Sunday when you do not believe in God.

No. None of this matters any more, for the first thing you learn here is that you do not matter at all. Indeed, it would be best for all concerned if you stopped existing altogether. Even though I am well-practiced in the art of self-immolation, the demands here are extreme. I must seal the door. Be still. Lights out.

Others develop their own survival strategies. My gentle sister becomes a witch. She now huddles over her desk in a black cloak, wide glasses, a steaming brew in her hand, muttering incomprehensible German gutterals to herself, hissing me off each time I approach. *Shsch. I am verking.*

I am left to wander through vaulted rooms charged with

a laughter translated into strangeness, the gossip of girls I do not understand. My language is awkward, techtonic, a clash of colonial, expatriate and tropical linguistic forms. What words can I offer to gain entry to the charmed circle of these ebullient, rosy-cheeked girls? I who have never heard of Status Quo, eaten Yorkshire pudding or worn tights before? I am tiny and brown. A curio, a talking toy. They lift their brown baby and coo. A parody of motherhood in a motherless land. And I, reduced to laughing at my humiliation, complicit in my diminution, stay silent and self-hating. I am not numb yet.

The first summer: drought and dry grass. The hottest on record. I am not conscious of heat, only of the tingling of my unwashed scalp and skin. Water is strictly rationed, like food, clothes, money, care. Then suddenly it begins to rain. Thin rain thickening into ropes of water lashing the tall flowers into hoops. We rush out with shampoo bottles and dance like gypsies, throwing our arms up to the sky. Feel the lust of running water on our faces and thighs.

That autumn there are ladybirds everywhere and the woods are wild with their red wings.

Her name is Rosamund. She is gentle as mist and has hair the colour of tamarind. She stands apart because she is at peace with herself and sees beauty about her where the rest of us feel anger and pain. I follow her, hungry for such peace, and listen as she lifts flowers into poetry. Weak yellow flowers, grizzled nuts, muddy shoots, gather in her hand and are baptised, granted name and lineage. Primrose and daffodil uncrumple as she calls them into being. I would not have noticed them but now they grow tall as Wordsworth. And who am I but a stranger in these woods?

I hold out my pinafore and feel the weight of hazelnuts she

pours in, lifted for a moment by the magic of these tumbling shells, before the cold wind bites and I run indoors.

People keep wanting to adopt me. Tall girls and the mothers of tall girls come up and ask with ice water in their eyes, *And when did you last see your parents?*

I have forgotten. I am forgetting what they look like. And I bristle at the insinuation that my parents are anything less than perfect. I can taste the smooth certainty of rich wine and plush carpets in their voice. They mean well but cannot understand the jungle that lies in me. Ours is a joint sacrifice, I tell myself, a trade-off of a bitter present for a better future. I can hear the elderly aunts from home with their faces drawn back into tight buns. *Your parents are working so hard to give you a good education. They are giving up a lot. You are such a lucky girl!*

They must love me very much to leave me. If I work hard enough and stay good, they might love me just a little bit more. My letters home are as shiny as Sunday shoes.

'And where did you learn to speak such good English?'
'Here, in England.'

I discover I am a great mimic and earn distinctions in elocution. I appear to be the perfect product of Macaulay's mission, having acquired the patina of English speech, manners and conduct. My cream-tea accent wins me social acceptance but the rewards of tasting the truth of words and feeling them ripen in my mouth, run much deeper. My voice becomes an instrument that catches melodies from air. I can look at a printed page and find a pulse in any piece, lift it into life at will. It is a sorcery that they wish to control. I duly give bible readings at the Baptist Church on Women's International Day and appear in regional French-speaking contests reciting Baudelaire; empty exercises performed to pacify. They feel secure in such ventriloquy and when they ask me to say something in my own language for a school play they seem to have won. All I remember are my prayers. Verses in Pali, the sacred language of the Sinhalese.

There I stand with my feathered headdress, transformed into the only Minnehaha in England who greets American rangers with a homage to the Buddha, the Dharma and the Sangha.

But a living language is an insurrection, beyond dominion and control, and the English that grows in me is an anarchic alphabet, a language to cross continents, to cradle hope, to cry and curse by. The real menace of mimicry is the violent eloquence of Caliban. For six years I serve an apprenticeship to poets of memory, loss, and thwarted desire, singing of their experiences, appearing to silence my own, little knowing that one day I will open my mouth and find a scream become a song.

ಳಿ

A land of contradictions where the sun is cold and day is night, where relatives are strangers and loneliness is an infectious disease. I, who have lived with contradictions all my life, know that, in a climate of sustained paradox, self-immolation can be the most effective form of self-preservation. Lose your self and it is impossible to feel anything.

The true story rests beyond articulation. Please be patient. I am doing my best to be understood. To dwell on the past requires us to inhabit it, to make memory a home, and I find I cannot live in this time now any more than I could then. How to make a home of a place defined by its loss? This is not my voice you hear, just the shape of an absence. A hole where my body might have been.

And there are those who cannot live with contradiction;

require clarity, singularity, coherence. They sail the horizon, skim the perfect edge and tip their wings towards the dark, free-falling. For them suicide is a linear act of will, pure and passionless as a sliding winter moon.

ε∞

Sybil is from East Africa, or so she has been told by her adoptive English parents. She is a year younger than I am and I do not notice her till she shuts herself in the dorm opposite mine, opens a window and threatens to throw herself out. Girls, staff, and firemen gather outside before she is finally coaxed back.

She is more careful the next time. Chooses a small music room on the fourth floor at a quiet hour, and eases herself into air. Her fall is broken by an abutment. She hits this and then lands further down by the drains, breaking her collarbone, both her legs, and tearing her spleen. They find her slippers aligned outside the door. She always was a tidy girl.

Helen is my warm and generous friend whose parents live in Zambia. She wants to be a nurse, has fallen in love with a Protestant priest and ministers to anyone in need. She's now passionate about a boy who likes to stroke her breasts but is not ready to care. One evening I find her hysterical, see the open bottle on the sill, and call for help.

It hurts, she says at the hospital, *when they suck your stomach clean.*

Petra is the most beautiful girl in my class - tall, tanned and blonde. She is bright, athletic, and blessed with a dashing brother and a home in Malta. Everybody wants to know her but she doesn't want to know herself. She gets thinner by the month. When her parents finally take her away, her wrists are as fine as the handle of her tennis racket, and her hair so full above her shrunken face that she appears to be wearing an oversized wig.

In the dark I open doors, stumble upon narrative, upon stories that are not mine to tell. I do not mean to intrude, wish to keep myself apart, protect myself from others' pain and grant them the privacy of their own, but find myself stumbling on, oblivious of boundary and redemption. Like the evening I walked alone to the boarding house, opened the broad oak door of Belvoir House and stepped into a shock of bright lights and Anne's broken screams.

All the senior officials are seated in the hall. They are gathered in a circle and Anne is screaming and pulling back, screaming and pulling back from a violence I can only measure from her response. The girls are gathered on the gallery above the stairs, out of range from all those below except for me, standing by the large open door with the cloak about my shoulders, a stray fragment of the night. I remove my shoes and hurry upstairs, join the watching girls.

'What is it? What's happened?'

'They have come to take Anne away.'

'Why?'

'Mrs Griffin found her in bed with Alison.'

'So?'

'Well, Mrs Griffin was walking her dogs and thought she heard something. She went to the window and saw Anne and Alison in bed together, kissing and that.'

'Where's Alison?'

'She is downstairs. They tried talking to her separately but she broke free and is with Anne. She's crying too. It's horrible.'

I am at the end of a huddle of girls, too far from the balustrade to see what is going on but don't need to, for they appear in my imagination, striding past on their way to the refectory, Anne and Alison, laughing and slipping their arms about one another. Two girls who shared breakfast, exchanged rings and confidences, whose staccato chatter and wild hoots of laughter splintered the greyness about us before it sealed us in again. Two girls who found warmth in the cold.

They left school that week in separate cars, leaving us to watch the thick door close.

ဆ

The sun is sick
Cold custard
The body a dead tree losing language like leaves
Grey walls seal the contradiction of
dim days and bright nights
into permanence
Forget the future
forgive the past
Seek solace in
the cellophane of ice

ဆ

And who do you like? asks Julie during art class.

I wrack my brain for a name, an image that will meet their requirements and remember a small picture of the Saint, or rather the actor who plays him, on the cover of one of my father's books. Also the TV series - hopelessly out-of-date though I wasn't aware of it at the time - featuring a slick, well-mannered and improbably good-looking Englishman whose name completely escapes me.

The Saint - from TV, I offer uncertainly.

Oh, you mean Roger Moore. He's James Bond now. Hey everyone, Noli fancies Roger Moore!

The girls stop painting and look at me with interest. I'm not sure if the name means any more to them than it does to me, but it is a man's name, an English man's name, and that must mean I am normal after all.

After that I am given a photo, then two more, of my new-found love and soon become inundated with magazine clippings, newspaper cuttings, posters and memorabilia with my hero's face on it, all brought by classmates who wish to nourish this nascent passion. I start a scrapbook and spend prep time cutting, pasting and pausing over the clippings like a lapidarist over prize butterflies. The pictures show an older but still striking man and I start wondering about this arranged match. I discover he is my mother's age, has been married three times and has three children, including a son who is slightly younger than me and who, I have decided, loves me madly. This is interesting because so, I discover, does his father and my nights are now spent in plush hotels and Hollywood parties making secret assignations between these two gorgeous beings. Then there is the mystery of the unknown first wife and an interview with an embittered second (whose focus of anger shifts between Roger's third - Italian - wife and myself) and rumours of rivalries and sudden reports of accidents which send me scurrying to his side and have me ministering to him as he lies in a shattered car professing his undying devotion as I drift off to a sleep as soothing as a warm kiss.

I remain faithful to Roger, despite his evident bigamy, till I leave school. The Bond films extend the vocabulary of my dreams and fill them with scintillating locations, outrageous plots and all manner of possible intersections for our different worlds. I am the dusky beauty who walks off the set and straight into his heart. My friends, who change boyfriends every month, wonder at my loyalty but it is not difficult. The sight of their acne-ridden lovers with shuffling feet, lank hair, bony chests and awkward fingers does nothing to entice me to switch partners. One girl returns proudly with a football shirt, another a leather wristband, and another a love-bite red as a plum, while I have sipped wine with Roger, cracked a code, dodged bullets in a field of opium poppies while holding tight to his hand, and end up being seduced in a catamaran off the coast of Vietnam. Naturally these global escapades leave me exhausted and I have little time or energy left for the conjugation of Latin verbs or the evaluation of the combustible properties of hydrochloric acid.

&

My brother who studies numerology, astrology and palmistry while reading politics, tells me, on one of our rare meetings, that I have a worrying head line. He peers at my hand, pressing the fingers back, and clicks his tongue on diagnosis. *Looks like Madness*, he declares, his brow, eyes and lips pulled into parallel arcs of consternation, *or* – and I hold my breath for a reprieve - *a Brain Tumour. You must be careful.*

I am too alarmed to ask precisely how I am to avoid my fate, and start to study my palms in earnest. Weigh up whether the large star on Saturn is mitigated by the striking constellation on Jupiter, count travel lines and squares of protection, read romance under my little finger and see dramatic possibilities on the double career line. It is certainly a complicated hand, with as much potential for wild success as for irredeemable disaster. It all depends on the translation.

Now that I have learnt to read the signs, the head line that sits like a squashed dragonfly on my palm continues to worry me.

I consult others who see in it the much more mundane (and I hope more probable) likelihood of *vulnerability to stress*, while the World Famous Clairvoyant of the East, Professor Mirza, who asked nothing of me beforehand, proclaims from his curtained cubicle by Brighton Pier, *A virile mind! Others think from A to B. You think from A to B, to PHD, to double PHD!!*

He looks as pleased as if he had received the honour himself.

I do not know whom to trust, who reads my future best, or whether it is entirely up to me to decode the pattern of my life.

ᴆ

In the days of slavery, the authorities created the carnival as a means of pacifying the slaves, giving them an official outlet for their frustration. In every institution that values regulation, rebellion, too, becomes ritualised. We were not aware of it at the time but our small misdemeanours had a history of official consent. In each midnight feast, every naked night swim, each frantic run to the boy's college in the dark, we were following a tradition of nocturnal rebellion that was accepted but not ignored; the token punishments of detention or standing in the cellar were themselves rituals that confirmed our bad behaviour. A criminal act demands the creativity of change. We become creative in our final years.

It is a tradition for those leaving the school to mark the event with small acts of rebellion in church on the last Sunday of term. Slamming hymn books on the floor, kissing the pew and stepping on the Methodist minister's toes when bidding adieu, are accepted by both the girls and their keepers as the right, however regrettable, of those who are about to be released. On these occasions, the headmistress, an elfin lady whose round spectacles transform her into Madame Tussaud, closely watches the gallery of girls above her during the service, and the unfortunate minister stands well back on the church steps and hides his wince behind the steeliest of Christian smiles. Afterwards, the most popular school leaver may be tossed into the pond on her way back from church.

The very best of us are leaving the fifth form - Miti, Elspeth, Fiona, Sue, Philippa and Bridget - and someone has been creative. It is our last Sunday together and we are in church. There has been a frenzy of book slamming pounding the gallery floor generating sharp glances from the headmistress while members of the public around her, wise to the ritual, pretend not to hear.

Now, as the organ strikes the opening chord, we rise as one body and open our mouths for the last hymn. The organ sets the pace and the congregation rounds its lips and launches into the first verse, *Oh Jesus I have promised*. At exactly the same moment we, dark shrouds of anonymity above, throw back our heads and with all the force that we can muster, storm into another, *Oh let me hear thee speaking*.

To serve thee to the end, trill Madame Tussaud and the waxworks below. *In accents clear and still*, we bellow thunderously against them, as girls from all the different forms join us and a hundred Aretha Franklins and Barbara Streisands roll into action like a hurricane over reeds. The public congregation below are barely audible, their thin dry notes snapping like twigs under the torrent from above, a rush of such power that it is crushing their words and shredding sense so only the odd chip of sound pokes through. *Ow, ear, ee.*

Above the storms of passion, we roar like Amazons at war, striding through the second verse while the huddle of souls, still confined to the first, skitter in the verbal deluge, missing words, logic, meaning, singing of objects without verbs, prepositions without subject, and in the babble, look up and lose their place on the page, make false starts, drop lines, grope for position, continuity, stability, while we charge on with the uncompromising gusto of those who know exactly where they are going, precisely what they are doing, delighting in our collective freedom, summoning the *murmur of self will* into a tropical crescendo of triumph, rolling on and on relentlessly, for the organ cannot stop, it must, like us, go through to the very end. And though some of us hold a longer hymn sheet than others and will remain here for two more years, we all know that one day it will end, that one day we will reach the last verse, the last term, and on that day we will open the door of this place, this place of stone where human contact is forbidden so that Mrs Griffin's parting embrace becomes the first hug I have had in years - melting me back into selfhood - we all know now, in a way we had never known before, that when we open the oak door, when we walk the stone steps, when we push the cloak off our shoulders and the sky comes down to lift us, we will raise our broken voices, make ribbons of the wind, and fork the land into thunder.

ACKNOWLEDGEMENTS

'The Breach' was first published in *Bridges: A Global Anthology of Short Stories ed.* Maurice A. Lee (2012) and was the Story of the Month in *The Missing Slate*, December 2013; 'The Map' was first published in *South Asian Review: Creative Writing Issue*, 29: 1, March 2009; 'The Dictionary of National Humiliation' was first published in *The Radiance of the Short Story: Fiction from Around the Globe* ed. Maurice A. Lee and Aaron Penn (2018); 'A Feast of Words' first appeared on-line on the English PEN website on 12 April, 2011; 'Breaking News'; 'Releasing Marius' and 'The Waves'; 'Getting to No'; and 'Heart' were first published in the following issues of *Wasafiri*: 75, Autumn 2013; 45, Summer 2005; 17, Spring 1993; 42: 20th Anniversary Special, Summer 2004; 'Too Many Legs' won an award in the Commonwealth Short Story Competition 2009 and was commercially produced on the CD 'Commonwealth Short Stories 2009: voices from our world' by the Commonwealth Foundation.

Minoli Salgado was born in Kuala Lumpur and grew up in Sri Lanka, South East Asia and England. Her novel, *A Little Dust on the Eyes* (2014), won the first SI Leeds Literary Prize and was longlisted for the DSC Prize in South Asian Literature. She is also the author of the critical study, *Writing Sri Lanka: Literature, Resistance and the Politics of Place* (2007). She is a Reader in English at the University of Sussex.